I0764481

GUILTY
UNTIL PROVEN GUILTY

Other books by Brian McNaughton

Fiction

The Throne of Bones
Downward to Darkness
Worse Things Waiting
Gemini Rising
Nasty Stories
Even More Nasty Stories
The House Across the Way
The Poacher
Riptide

GUILTY
UNTIL PROVEN GUILTY

Brian McNaughton

BETANCOURT
& COMPANY
Doylestown, Pennsylvania

In 1979, Carlyle Communications published a related but substantially different book by this title.

Guilty Until Proven Guilty
A publication of
Betancourt & Company, Publishers
P.O. Box 45
Gillette, NJ 07933-0045

www.wildsidepress.com

SECOND EDITION

Chapter One

When you leave Armitage by the east end of town, crossing an old cantilever bridge by the Burroughs Thread Company, the hills seem to rise straight up to meet you. The natives call these hills mountains, although the biggest of them falls short of 2,500 feet. The view from the First World War monument at the top of Mt. Amos is rewarding, if you like picture postcard views of New England, and if you can ignore the industrial area in the foreground, dominated by the red-brick mill and its railroad sidings.

The hills are heavily wooded. Viewing them from the town, it's hard to believe that they were ever otherwise. When you walk through them, though, you find overgrown traces of wagon-roads, stone fences that once marked out fields, and rectangular depressions that used to be the cellars of snug little farmhouses. There is a neglected graveyard in which the name Burroughs is prominent among the remnants of the slate headstones. The mill had made huge profits from uniforms during the Civil War, but Amos Burroughs miscalculated that the war would last a few years longer than it did. In the local depression that followed, most of the farmers pulled up stakes and went West.

Several waves of immigrants have washed through Armitage since then: Italians, Slavs, French Canadians, Southern blacks. Whenever one group would settle down and begin talking about a living wage, the Burroughses would look for a replacement group. Most recently, the Puerto Ricans have been giving way to the Vietnamese.

All of the groups have left settlers behind them, people who were ingenious enough to find work outside the mill or start their own businesses, and the thread company is no longer the town's only employer. Since the construction of the interstate highway, which connects with the road that wanders through the hills on the east, many people who commute to larger cities have moved in. Most of them live in garden apartment complexes with fanciful names on the western outskirts of town. The town's second-largest employer is a relatively new branch of the state university.

One of the professors at the university caused a national stir – and a local tempest – by writing a sociological study of Armitage, in which he pointed out that the town has one of the highest rates of violent crime per capita in the United States. Skillfully avoiding actionable libel, he implicitly blamed the Burroughs family for its old strategy of pitting one ethnic group against another. He suggested that the town's traditionally drunken, violent Saturday nights were a direct result of the dull work and low wages at the mill.

The *Armitage Advertiser* editorialized that the professor, for suggesting that the townspeople were anything but happy, progressive, and law-abiding, should be ridden out of town on a rail. The slur was eventually refuted by Police Chief Willard C. Hoskins, who pointed out that the crime rate wasn't really higher in

Armitage than anywhere else; the disparity was due to the efficiency of his police department, which investigated and reported crimes that were ignored in other towns.

Despite the prosperity and increasing population of the town, the chief ambition of anyone who had been raised in Armitage was to get out of it. Melody Boisvert and Bill Oates shared that ambition, and they had gone up to the World War monument one hot Saturday night in July to discuss it.

The old roads and firelanes through the hills, and most particularly the area around the monument, had once attracted many young couples on Saturday nights. Bill and Melody saw no parked cars that night. They supposed this was due to concern about the rapist – "The Full Moon Maniac," the *Advertiser* called him, although only one of his attacks had occurred *exactly* on a night of a full moon – who had struck three times in the past eighteen months. He preyed on couples in lovers' lanes, locking the man in the trunk of a car while he forced the woman to commit what the *Advertiser* called "unnatural acts." On the last occasion, a young man named John Evans had been shot to death. But the Full Moon Maniac had been inactive now for more than six months.

"He must've been a kid at the college," Bill said, echoing a popular theory. "See, the last time was right during midterm exams. The heat got too much for him, he was worried about flunking and all, so he went nuts and ran out to tear off a piece."

"I wish you wouldn't talk like that, Bill," Melody said, pulling against his encircling arm.

"*I'm* not talking like that!" he protested. "I'm talking like the way a nut like that would think about it. I mean, somebody who really cares for somebody else, like the way I care for you, I wouldn't think about it like that."

"Don't think about it at all, huh?" she said, making a token struggle when he put his hand on her breast.

She felt a flutter inside when he kissed her. It came on more quickly this time, and it threatened to be stronger than usual. She escaped his kiss, her lips rubbing his cheek. The scratch of the stubble that he never completely succeeded in eliminating cooled her slightly.

Bill pulled away and got up from their granite seat. He walked away from the monument with stiff, jerky steps.

"You don't realize what this does to a guy, Melody," he choked. "I mean, I *hurt.* It's like a real pain."

"Well, I'm sorry. But what you want to do, I know what *that* does to a girl."

He came back quickly and knelt in front of her, his forearms resting on her knees. His blue eyes, adapted to the night, were like big, dark pools, and she felt as if she might drown in them. A feeling like a pleasant dizziness tingled through her.

"Well, there are ways, you know. I mean, like this is like the twentieth century and all," he said earnestly.

She found it hard to refute his logic. The Pope to the contrary notwithstanding, she saw nothing intrinsically wrong with birth control. Obtaining the means was the problem. She could never in a million years go to Dr. LaPlante, who had brought her into the world. That Jewish doctor on High Street would probably do it without a single question, but she couldn't stand the thought of him snickering behind her back afterward. He would make a joke to his nurse about Catholic hypocrites who came to him for only one reason.

And when he fitted her for one of those things and found out – that she was a virgin – no, the whole thing was unthinkable.

But even more unthinkable, now that Bill's hands had slipped under her skirt and were caressing her bare thighs, was the thought of remaining a virgin very much longer. At seventeen, she felt like a freak, the only one of her kind in the country – although, in cooler moments, she knew that most of the talk she'd heard from the other girls at St. Denis's had been only that, just talk.

"You know, guys can take precautions, too," he murmured, his lips moving against the skin of her thigh. "Like I'm prepared, in case . . ."

He had slipped his fingers inside her panties. This was the point where she always stopped him. She had always found the strength before by summoning up a mental image of Monsignor Fagan, bald and doddering, who could suddenly transform himself into the Spanish Inquisition if you mentioned sex. "How far did he insert his finger?" he had actually asked her once, and she dreaded the possibility of running into him in the confessional. Father Corelli, who was young and handsome and tried to keep up with the latest slang, would accept her admission of "impure acts" and let it go at that.

The meaning of Bill's words suddenly hit her like a splash of cold water. She wrenched his hand away and jerked her skirt down. God! How he could he be so unfeeling, so sleazy? He wanted to taker her virginity with a . . . with a *rubber,* for God's sake!

He muttered something that she ignored. She turned away from him and looked at the town below. It looked much bigger at night. In the daytime, you didn't notice the new apartments in the lower hills on the other side of the valley, but at night their lights were visible. Armitage used to have only the faults of a provincial town, but now it combined them with those of suburbia. She was glad she would be going away to college in the fall. And Bill would join the Navy. They'd probably never see each other again after this summer. They would grow into different people, with different interests. So what did it matter, really? She wanted to say yes. If only he would go about it the right way!

"Bill . . ." She didn't know how to continue. She seized on a lucky distraction as a rift appeared in the low clouds. "Look! It's a full moon."

"No, it isn't," he grumbled. "Not for two days yet. I looked it up."

She reached out and stroked his wiry blond hair. Encouraged, he moved closer and put his hand almost as high as it had been before.

"I thought you weren't afraid of the Maniac," she said.

"I'm not. Like I said, I figure he flunked out of college and went back to wherever he came from. Or else killing that guy shook him up so much that he decided to quit. What I'm afraid of is, on the night of the full moon, this place would be crawling with newspaper reporters and cops."

He was trying to peel her panties down, but he couldn't manage it because she was sitting on them. If she raised herself even slightly it would be an invitation. She raised herself.

"Oh, Melody."

The granite felt cold under her naked skin. She leaned back against the monument and closed her eyes. She let her thighs drift apart under the gentle pressure of his hands.

"Oh, no, Bill, please don't do that! I can't stand it! It's – oh, no!"

"Take your sweater off," he mumbled, and his lips moved now against the softest and most sensitive flesh of all.

She hesitated for only a moment, then fumbled with the buttons. He hadn't mentioned her bra; but, after a moment's thought, she took that off, too, while he pulled down her skirt.

This was crazy – out here in the middle of a clearing in the moonlight. They should have gone back to the car, or at least into the darkness of the surrounding woods. But things had happened so fast.

She kept her eyelids open only just enough to watch him struggle out of his pants. She had never seen an erect penis before. It scared her. It was bigger than she had imagined; nor had she ever dreamed that it would be such an ugly-looking thing. She reached out and touched it.

"Don't use . . . anything, Bill. Do it like this."

"I don't know."

He leaned over her, standing between her legs as he kissed her breasts. She knew that she couldn't have been the first for him. He was too gentle and skillful and slow. She lay all the way back on the cold stone as her nipples tingled and hardened almost painfully.

"Don't stop," she said. "Why did you stop?"

She opened her eyes and screamed.

Small and skinny and naked, Bill seemed to have been half-absorbed into a huge dark bulk, a congealed shadow. His eyes stared, his mouth hung open. A hand gripped his hair. The barrel of a gleaming black gun was jammed into his ear. Even at the moment it seemed to her a foolish and irrelevant thing to notice, but she saw that his penis was no longer erect.

"Don't scream again, or I'll kill him," said a muffled voice. The man was wearing a ski-mask: more properly, a knitted *toque* with crudely cut eyeholes.

"Don't – you're hurting me," Bill said, and then he let out a strangled cry as the gun-barrel was twisted viciously in his ear.

"I'll fuck you up the ass with it, you dirty little prick, and then I'll pull the trigger. How would you like that?"

"No. Please. No!"

Melody didn't know where the words came from, but they were forced from her lips by a burst of rage: "Stop hurting him, you pervert!" The man laughed. "You stop hurting when you're dead and buried, cunt. You want that for him?"

The strength of her anger had left her. Clutching a bunch of discarded clothes to her breasts, pressing her legs together, she could only shake her head.

"Get up."

She did as he told her, but her legs shook so violently that standing was an effort. She felt as if she might faint. She prayed silently that she would.

"Go to your car."

She turned to snatch up her shoes and the rest of her clothing.

"Never mind!" he barked. "You won't need them."

The cops would arrive, they were closing in now: that's what she told herself as she stumbled barefoot through the grass, a step ahead of Bill and the man who held him. The newspaper said they were the best and toughest department in the state. They were looking for the Full Moon Maniac, weren't they? It stood to reason that they would have men in hiding up here on the nights close to the full moon.

She remembered a policeman, a detective, who had come to speak to one of her classes at St. Denis a couple of years ago. He had red hair – not the coarse, frizzy kind, but a gleaming red helmet, neatly cut in layers and covering his ears and his collar. He'd looked more like a rock star than a cop. His face had been lean and handsome, with tense lines around the mouth and eyes, but his smile had made her go all quivery inside. His blue blazer had been casually unbuttoned to permit exciting glimpses of two guns, one at his hip and a bigger one under his arm. His lecture had been the usual dumb nonsense about drugs that everybody knew already, but the girls had listened breathlessly to every word. He was terribly old, of course, but nobody had been able to talk about anything else but him for weeks afterward. Somebody told her that he'd shot and killed eight men in the line of duty. He was waiting in the woods, she knew it. He would step out and shoot this dirty, motherfucking, son-of-a-bitching bastard!

"Get the keys."

They had reached Bill's father's Pontiac, parked lopsidedly in an old dirt road that was nothing more than a pair of weed-choked ruts. He had checked it out while they were .at the monument, he knew that the keys were in the ignition: something about that detail frightened her more than anything she had yet experienced.

She went forward around the car. It occurred to her that it had been foolish to keep clutching her clothes to her breasts while the man had been walking behind her. She switched them to cover her buttocks.

"Just drop them. And if you want him dead, just try running away. You won't get far, either, not with bare feet."

She hadn't even thought about that. She might make it. She had long, strong legs; she could outrun most men. Would he risk shooting Bill, alerting anyone who might be within earshot, then come blundering after her in the woods? Maybe not; but she didn't have the right to gamble with Bill's life that way.

Bill's life: for the first time it struck her that this creep might actually kill them. She couldn't die, not tonight! Her sister Debbie's twelfth birthday was next week; and she hadn't begun to prepare the party she'd planned, she hadn't even bought Debbie a present yet. Even worse, she'd given her mother a short answer to some harmless question on her way out the door tonight. That might be the last word she would ever speak to her mother.

The unspeakable injustice of it rekindled her anger, but she channeled it into a hard, clear line. She would do exactly what he told her. She would do and say nothing that might touch off his madness. But she would memorize every detail, every word he spoke, every nuance of tone and gesture. Mask or not, she would identify him when they caught him, and her testimony would put him in a cell for the rest of his life.

She obeyed him and dropped her clothing. When she returned to the back of the car with the keys, she tried to shield herself with her hands. But he was looking at Bill, muttering in his ear.

"I'm going to fuck your girl friend, kid. Do you want to make something out of it? Do you? Good. I didn't think so. You be a good boy, you behave yourself, and I'll let you have sloppy seconds while I watch. I'll make her give you a blowjob. Would you like that?"

Bill squeezed his eyes shut and said nothing. When she got close enough, she saw that he was shaking as badly as she was, and he was crying. Her heart went out to him. She wanted to tell the man that he was a coward and a bully; that, without his mask and gun, he would probably scurry into the woodwork if anybody stood up to him. But she remembered her resolution and kept her mouth shut.

"Give him the keys, cunt. Open your trunk, kid."

The key rattled against the metal of the trunk-lock as Bill fumbled to fit it in. The lid sprang up. The man pushed Bill inside and slammed the lid. She was alone with him. He gripped her by the wrist and pulled her into the shadows.

She couldn't see him very well here, but she had

gotten a good look at him before. He was big, he seemed like the biggest man she had ever seen in her life, but she suspected that he was thin. His bulk came from his heavy clothing, inappropriate for the weather. His hands, big and bony, were stark white against his dark clothes.

He made her lean over a fallen tree and spread her legs. The rough bark hurt her stomach. He gripped her hair in one hand and pushed the gun against her chin with the other. She felt his hot, hard flesh rubbing against her buttocks. Whenever she screamed, he would twist her hair until that pain was even worse than the pain below.

A long time passed. When he had exhausted the inventiveness of his sick mind, he dragged her to the trunk and shoved her in with Bill. The trunk now had a foul odor.

The man laughed. "He shit himself, the silly little bastard. What are you doing with a wimp like this?"

She sobbed, unable to speak. She felt an emotion that was almost like happiness: it was over, the worst had happened, they, were going to live. If only he would go!

"Disgusting little pig gives great head, I'll say that for her. You ought to check it out while you're waiting to get rescued, kid."

The lid of the trunk slammed, the lock clicked. There was no air. The odor was overpowering. Her limbs were twisted painfully, jammed against Bill's, and neither of them could move. A sour taste filled her mouth. She fought against it, but soon she was throwing up and struggling for air.

Bill shouted, making her ears ring: "You'll never get a trial, cocksucker! When they catch you, I'm going to come and kill you!"

She jabbed him with her elbow, trying to shut him

up. What in the holy name of God was he trying to prove? They weren't safe yet. The Maniac could open the trunk as easily as he'd closed it. But Bill wouldn't stop shouting and sobbing threats.

A noise like an explosion with clanging, metallic overtones deafened her. At the same time she saw the dull glow of the sky through a ragged hole in the lid of the trunk. She couldn't understand why a hole should suddenly, miraculously open in the trunk, giving her the air she so desperately craved.

She heard a second explosion, a second hole appeared, and she understood.

Chapter Two

When Detective Sergeant Frank Buchanan arrived on the scene, the volunteer firemen were standing around in their slickers and gumboots, drinking beer. A couple of them were methodically hosing down the woods, which had been burned in a thirty-yard-wide area. The woods were damp from recent rain, so a forest fire had been averted.

"Can't we get these clowns out of here?" he asked Jack Grenier, the first uniformed policeman he saw.

The cop shrugged. "We need their generator. For the lights."

Frank had overlooked that, and the oversight annoyed him. "We don't need all of them. Move them back."

He went to the skeleton of the Pontiac. The lid of the trunk was up. Inside were a couple of things that looked like twisted statues of monkeys made of charcoal. They didn't look nearly big enough to have been people. The hairless, featureless heads were round, vaguely simian. One of them showed its teeth. A white bone gleamed in a black thigh.

It used to give Frank nightmares, the way people,

seemingly so solid and well put together, could be torn or burned or redistributed all over the landscape by the right combination of unexpected circumstances. Such sights used to remind him forcibly how vulnerable his own flesh and bones were. After he'd shot his second or third man, he no longer had nightmares. There were people who did things, and there were people who let things happen to them, and he knew he would never, be a victim.

Dr. Goodwin, the medical examiner, came up with a smelly black cigar jammed in his unshaven face. He smoked cigars only at crime scenes and *post mortem* examinations. They were his defense against the odors of death and corruption. He had fallen out of bed into a sweat shirt and jeans.

"What can you tell me?" Frank asked.

"He fired six times through the lid of the trunk. One of the shots ruptured the gas tank. Either the muzzle-blast touched off the gasoline, or else he lit a match. I figure he used a revolver, like always. There are no cartridge casings lying around." Having indulged his passion for playing detective, Goodwin touched briefly on his own ground: "What killed them, maybe I can tell you after I post them."

Frank recalled how, as a young cop, he had pictured the medical examiner mailing bodies away to unspecified destinations.

"You can't tell me whether she was raped."

The M.E. took out his cigar and laughed as he pointed with it. "That one is *she*, I think, but I doubt that I'll be able to tell you much more about her."

"What color were they?" Frank asked.

"Are you kidding?" He looked at Frank oddly and asked, "What difference does it make?"

Frank smiled sourly. There was no point in explaining, because Goodwin knew the answer. Middle-class whites would attract news coverage from the cities, especially if the victims were kids and not aging adulterers; blacks or Puerto Ricans would be lucky to make the front page of the *Advertiser.*

Frank strolled around the car. The tires had melted away; the upholstery had burned to the springs. It would be nice to find a clue for a change. He had never found a clue, nor ever heard of anyone finding one, at a real-life murder scene. You closed cases by shaking people until something fell out. Nevertheless, the state police laboratory people were on their way here to look for clues.

An electronic flash glared behind him, and he turned. It was only the police photographer from his own department.

He was glad the call had reached him while he was out on a date. His clothes were pressed, his hair had been trimmed that morning, he was clean shaven. He wouldn't have wanted to turn up in the pages of a big-city newspaper looking like the medical examiner. He wasn't sorry that his date had been interrupted, either. Angelique was thirty-five, her tits sagged, and her ass was too big, but she was very enthusiastic in bed. She'd been getting difficult lately. She had insisted on going to the French Club, a place where Frank normally wouldn't be caught dead; because it was the sort of place where that just might happen. The club had been converted from an old factory, and the floor rested on massive springs that had once supported heavy machinery. As the evening wore on and the French Canadians lost their inhibitions, the floor would start bouncing like the deck of a ship in a storm under their Frankenstein boots. The place was good for at least one knifing or bottle-carving a week. Everybody there knew Frank, hated his guts, and resented the fact that he was with one of their women, so he had fortunately stayed cold sober.

The forest warden who had reported the fire showed up, and Frank interviewed him. He learned only that the warden had spotted the fire from his tower at two-fifteen a.m. He was annoyed that someone should incinerate people in his woods, running the risk of a forest fire. Frank was grateful for the interruption when another uniformed cop came up from the paved road below.

"We got a make on the vehicle," he said, slighting none of the syllables in the last word. The cop's name was Ronnie Elkins; at twenty-five, he was forty pounds overweight.

"Yeah?"

"The vehicle is registered to William T. Oates, Sr., who owns the hardware store on Benefit Street?" He made a question of it, so Frank nodded. "He loaned the car to his son, William T., Jr., age seventeen, last night. Junior picked up a girl named Melody Boisvert, also seventeen, at eight o'clock."

Ronnie pronounced the girl's name *"Boyce*-vert," which was a dumb mistake for an Armitage cop to make. Frank knew he would never make a detective.

"Senior is on his way to identify the bodies," Ronnie said.

"Whose bright idea was that?"

"I don't know. I'm just telling you what I got on the radio."

"Okay. Your job will be to stand down there at the bottom of this dirt road and make sure he doesn't come up here. And get rid of all these other civilians on your way down. Find out if they heard any shots."

The area of the fire had filled up with sightseers, and none of the firemen had left yet. Ronnie looked at them doubtfully, confused by his responsibility.

"What will I tell Senior?"

"Christ, tell him they're not done yet," Frank said, then added hastily, "No. Let me know when he gets here; I'll talk to him."

"What do I do if somebody heard shots?"

Frank took a deep breath and looked at his Gucci loafers, now crusted with muddy ashes. "Take his name and address."

Frank turned and walked away. Bellowing orders, Ronnie advanced on the crowd. The firemen laughed.

"Michael J. Ryan is here," Patrolman Grenier reported, naming a local undertaker.

Frank sighed. No newsmen had arrived yet, and they would be disgruntled if they missed the bodies. Then he saw that Joe Spina from the *Advertiser* was on the scene.

"Tell Ryan not to waste any time; some relatives are on the way. Where's Dr. Goodwin?"

"He left twenty minutes ago."

"Lazy son-of-a-bitch, I wanted him to post them tonight. Okay, get Ryan organized."

Frank approached Joe Spina, who was taking pictures of the back of the car with a Rolleiflex.

"Who are those for, the *National Enquirer*?"

"Fuck it. I take the pictures, they say, 'We can't use this shit.' I don't take the pictures, they say, 'Where's the pictures?'"

"Hang around. Ryan is going to wrap them up nice for you."

"Stand over here by the side and look disapproving, Frank. I'll take your picture. Beautiful. No, wait a minute. I can't take your picture like that, Frank. Where's your carnation?" He snapped the picture at the moment he expected Frank to laugh, but Frank didn't. "One more."

The firemen helped Ryan and his assistant transfer the bodies to wicker baskets. Frank supervised the emptying of the trunk, still hoping for clues. He still didn't see any.

"Which one does this arm belong with?" a fireman asked.

"What difference does it make?" Ryan asked. "Let the medical examiner figure it out; that's his job. Anyway, that's a leg."

Joe Spina interviewed Frank as the bodies were carried away. Frank had been burned by the press a hundred times and he distrusted them profoundly, but he tried never to show it.

The excitement died down. No more reporters showed up. Neither did the mayor or Chief Hoskins or even Capt. LaPlante, as Frank had expected. Maybe they thought that this could be played down, that the Full Moon Maniac would go away if they ignored him. He was bad for business, after all. Parents would think twice about sending their kids to the state college in Armitage.

He took a walk up to the First World War Monument. The sky was already getting light in the east, and he spotted the clothing near the monument as soon as he came out of the woods. He examined it with the aid of his flashlight. A colorful, peasant-type skirt and a pair of panties that Angelique could only have used for a handkerchief. Tiny sandals. He had made her walk back to the car in her bare feet. The boy's wallet was in his jeans, confirming the identification. The wallet held a packet of three condoms and a twenty-dollar bill.

He found the girl's purse. It contained a wallet full of kids' pictures, ten dollars and change, an ID from St. Denis Roman Catholic High School. The picture on the ID showed a pretty, dark-haired girl with a roundish face and almond eyes. She looked familiar. He had probably seen her at one of his Mickey Mouse drug lectures.

Up until now, Frank had felt no emotion toward the Full Moon Maniac. He was just another scumbag who had to be stopped in one way or another, no more to be hated than a rat or a cockroach. Looking at the girl's picture and remembering her earnest face clearly now, he felt a cold rage take hold of him.

He sat on the monument and looked at the town. The bright pattern of the streets was empty now; few lights shone in the houses. One of them was shining in the Boisvert home, certainly, and in the Oates home. Maybe one of the lights belonged to the Maniac, staying up to celebrate.

When he caught him, Frank believed, he would find him in the college. The students were under the kind of intense pressure that aggravates quirks and instabilities; being young, many of them didn't know how to handle it. And, unlike most people under pressure, they had time on their hands. They kept odd hours; they came and went as they pleased. He had already shaken a number of people at the college, and nothing had fallen out. He was no longer welcome on campus.

After the third rape – the third reported rape, which meant it might have actually been the tenth or twelfth rape – he had begun thinking about the kid who had terrorized the Ann Arbor campus in Michigan: a boy-next-door type, caught by accident. That seemed to be the only way such people were ever caught. Nobody would ever know for sure whether the Boston Strangler had been identified. Jack the Ripper had never been caught.

Of course, you could make accidents happen sometimes. For four consecutive months, around the night of the full moon, he had prowled the hills on his own time without success. He'd finally decided there was no percentage in it, that the rapist had probably left town, and now two more kids were dead. At least they were white, that was one thing to be thankful for, he thought bitterly.

Catching the Maniac had become a hobby, and the hobby threatened to become an obsession. It had nothing to do with Frank's hatred for the rapist or detestation of his crimes: up until now, he hadn't felt any. It had more to do with himself, with the direction – or lack of it – in his own life. He could be decisive and energetic in small decisions, but he had always left the big ones to drift. He had pissed away fifteen years of his life in the Armitage Police Department, and he had nothing to look forward to but a detective lieutenancy when Chief Hoskins retired – which would be soon – and LaPlante was promoted to that job.

He was thirty-eight years old now, and that was too old to switch careers. He believed that he was highly intelligent, very aggressive, and that he could be charming when he needed to be – but whatever his abilities, who wanted an old cop from East Armpit Junction for any kind of job but security guard?

A few years back, while pasting clippings in his thick scrapbook, it had occurred to him that he ought to run for public office. The newspapers considered him colorful copy; they had taken to referring to him as "Armitage's dapper detective," alternating that with Frank "Two-Gun" Buchanan. His services as a speaker were in demand at the local clubs and schools. Chief Hoskins took him along to police conventions, where other police officers recognized him by his face or reputation. People seemed to like him.

He had approached the county's Democratic boss and suggested that he might run for city councilman. The boss, known for his pungent comments, said: "You don't run for office in a bleeding-heart state with eight dead men hanging around your neck."

So much for politics. It had done no good to explain that all eight of them had been armed, that he had been fully exonerated in each case, and that every last one of those scumbags had richly deserved it. The boss had reminded him of that infamous sociological study, in which the pipsqueak professor noted that Armitage had one of the few police departments in the country that boasted a public executioner.

But since then the tide had begun to turn.

Even the bleeding hearts had grown tired of bleeding real blood. People wanted the death penalty. Failing that, they wanted police officers who could circumvent the law to achieve justice. When the details of the Boisvert-Oates killing got out, would the public applaud the policeman who found the killer, read him his rights, and lead him off to hold hands with a psychiatrist? Or would they applaud Frank Buchanan, who planned to catch him, and who, upon catching him, would squash him, like a bug?

Having done that, he could run for governor while the county boss begged permission to kiss his ass. Or, if he set his sights lower, he could breeze past LaPlante into Hoskins's chair. That might be the smart move. A police chief would carry more weight in a gubernatorial race than a detective sergeant; a police chief whose autobiography was a bestseller, whose name was a household word like Wyatt Earp or Popeye Doyle.

He found that he was staring at the light in the Burroughs mansion on High Street. There was no justice in that. With all his talents and virtues, here he sat spinning fantasies on a cold rock while an asshole like Walter Burroughs owned the town. He owned it for no other reason than that he had been born into the right family. While hired managers ran it for him, he played with toy trains in his basement. Or played with his wife in the bedroom. He had married an elegant beauty with odd taste in clothes who had always fascinated Frank. Slim, with high cheekbones, fair skin, and straight, black hair, she resembled Hollywood's notion of an Indian princess, and she dressed the part. She was the kind of woman, Frank knew, who would lose interest in him the minute she calculated his salary. He didn't know whether that told him more about women or about money. He knew it didn't tell him anything about the rapist, so he gathered up the clothing and walked back the way he had come. He looked for footprints as he walked, but he didn't find any.

"Am I under arrest?"

Frank looked blankly at the angry man Bonnie Elkins was restraining. He was large and bald and distraught, and for a moment before he recognized him, Frank had the sick feeling that Ronnie had somehow managed to arrest the Full Moon Maniac.

"You're Sgt. Buchanan, aren't you?" the man demanded.

"Yes, but what. . . ?"

"This Gestapo agent has been holding me here for half an hour to talk to you. I want to get to the hospital to see my son."

Frank cleared his throat and glared at Bonnie, who continued to look proud of himself. "I'm sorry, Mr. Oates. You don't need to make a personal identification."

"I want to see him."

"Look, the hospital will release him to whatever funeral director you want tomorrow, after Dr. Goodwin has completed his examination. You can."

"I don't want a goddamn funeral director, I want to see Bill –"

"There's nothing to see," Frank cut in sharply. "He was burned beyond recognition."

While Oates was digesting that, Frank separated the boy's clothing from the girl's. "Were these his?"

The anger seemed to drain out of the bald man. He nodded. "He was wearing them last night. When he went to see that dirty little Canuck slut. I told him. . . ." He looked away.

Frank managed to swallow the rebuke that came to his lips as Oates turned and walked back down the dirt road. He saw no point in telling Ronnie off, either. He noticed that Bonnie was making a disorganized attempt to look like a soldier at attention, and Frank looked down the road to see Capt. LaPlante approaching. The captain was a gray-maned, athletic man in his forties who didn't smoke or drink. If he replaced Hoskins, he would be chief forever; and he didn't care much for Frank or his methods.

A few days ago, Frank had been telling the captain and some others at headquarters about a movie on television that he'd greatly enjoyed called *Dirty Harry.* Although he'd found it unbelievable in spots and phony at times, he'd been enthusiastic about its message: that a cop should sometimes cut through red tape to get the job done. LaPlante and the others had seemed vaguely embarrassed by his praise of the movie, and someone had abruptly changed the subject.

He now recognized the people who were coming up the path with the captain. One of them was a stringer for the Associated Press, the others were a reporter and a photographer for a city newspaper. Apparently tipped by LaPlante, they left him abruptly to pursue William Oates, Sr.

"What have you got?" LaPlante said, and Frank told him.

The captain listened, nodding occasionally, as he prowled around the hulk of the car. When Frank had finished, he said, "I hear you were at the French Club last night."

"Yeah, my favorite bar."

"Well, they had a knifing there after you left. Since you were there, I figure you're the best man to handle it." LaPlante took the bundle of clothing from Frank's hands. "I'll take charge of this case myself."

Chapter Three

"We having TV dinners again, hon?"

Katy Burroughs's fingers whitened on the handle of the refrigerator door as she tried to will away the knot that gripped her stomach. The knot formed often when Walter spoke to her nowadays. If only he'd make a forthright complaint about her choice of food! But he couldn't do anything forthrightly. He chose an exasperating middle ground in his tone that was half a complaint and half a whining apology.

"The Library Society meets tonight. You, know that," she said. "I don't have time for anything else. And if you don't like what I give you, why don't you hire a cook? God knows we can afford it."

Walter prowled around the edges of the big kitchen, seeking the shadows, like a tame bear who doesn't want to attract the full attention of its trainer. "Servants are a pain in the ass," he muttered. "The maid is bad enough, all the time prying into my things. I can never find anything when she's been cleaning my study. Servants want to run your whole damned life. They think they own the place, and the people who live in a house are just a nuisance they have to put up with.

That's the way it was when I was growing up, and I swore to God I wasn't going to spend the rest of my life being pushed around by servants. Anyway, what could we get? Some stupid nigger who'd poison us by mistake; you can't get a white person to be a servant anymore."

Katy had heard all this before. She'd heard it long before, way back in high school, when it had seemed the touching plea of a sensitive young man imprisoned by material possessions. Now it drove her mad with rage and frustration. It was like being forced to listen, every day of her life, to some insipid nursery jingle that had charmed her as a child.

"Maybe it wouldn't hurt to skip the Library Society for once," he said. "It seems like you're never home anymore."

"Why should I stay home? Is there something good on television?" she asked, but she knew the sarcasm would be lost on Walter.

"As a matter of fact, one of my favorites: *Dead Reckoning*, with Humphrey Bogart and Lizabeth Scott. It's one of the watersheds of the *film noir,*" he said, drawing on the jargon of the movie books that were his favorite reading. "But that's not on until later."

"I've been looking forward to this evening, Walter," she said. "Professor Swift is going to discuss Tolkien."

"Oh," said Walter, as if he knew who Tolkien was.

On a perverse impulse, she tried to frustrate her own plans by saying: "It wouldn't hurt you to go. You might learn something."

"I've got some stuff to do in the basement," he said. "Some other time, maybe."

Katy smiled to herself, for once pleased with her ability to predict everything her husband would say. She didn't know what she would have done if he'd agreed to accompany her. After long soul-searching she had finally decided to let Quentin Swift get what he was after, and she was going to spring the surprise on him after the meeting tonight. In his own way Quentin was as dull and predictable as Walter; but at least he wanted her. She felt a tingling sensation, partly guilt and partly anticipation, as she thought about her plans for the evening.

"Is it the Polynesian kind?" Walter asked hopefully as he tiptoed up to peer over her shoulder at the oven.

"No, German. Sauerbraten and red cabbage and noddles."

"I like the Polynesian kind," Walter sighed.

It made her wince, the way he pronounced that word, even after she'd corrected him a dozen times. That was probably his most annoying habit: stubbornly flaunting his ignorance, even when he really wasn't all that ignorant. It made it impossible for her to take Walter anywhere, or to invite any of the worthwhile people over for parties. They all thought Walter was a bad joke. That was just fine with him, of course, and that was probably why he acted the way he did. To his credit, he also turned away visits and resisted invitations from the snobs and chiselers and social climbers who begged for the chance to be bored by him.

He couldn't really be blamed for being the way he was. His father had been an unperceptive, unfeeling tyrant who had somehow conceived the fixed idea that his son was totally inept, probably a half-wit, and had always treated him as such. He could have sent Walter to the finest private school in the country, and Walter probably would have done well at it; but, on the grounds that the money would have been wasted, he sent his son to Armitage High.

Walter was shy and unsociable. His father had convinced him of his inferiority. He had no talent for sports and shared none of his contemporaries' outside interests. And his father was the unpopular boss of most of the other fathers in town. Consequently the other kids made life hell for him. They jeered at him, mocked him, made him the butt of cruel jokes; he was beaten up at least once a week for four years. Katy had been his only friend in school. Pity had attracted her, but he had opened up to her sympathetic interest, he had shown her a side that he showed no one else, and she had fallen in love with him.

Despite all his handicaps he did well in high school, and he could have been admitted to college, but his father refused to send him. Even though the old man had gone to Harvard, and his father and grandfather before him, he claimed that a college education was unnecessary. He insisted that his son learn the family business from the ground up, and he set him to work pushing a broom at the mill.

Katy had hoped to continue her education, but she had no money. She was working in a five-and-ten, trying to save some, when Walter asked her to marry him. They eloped, and the old man went crazy with rage. He tried to buy her off with twenty thousand a year for the rest of her life. He threatened to cut Walter out of his will. Neither one of them cared about the money. They were perfectly happy in their rented trailer.

At least the old man didn't fire Walter, but he didn't promote him, either, and Walter was still pushing a broom when the old man dropped dead three years later.

They had expected the elder Burroughs to live forever. He was a huge, vital, energetic man, a superhuman ogre. They were unprepared for the consequences of his death, both the wealth and the responsibilities. Entering the huge old house for the first time, Katy had felt like some fairy-tale waif who inherits an enchanted palace.

But that had been a long time ago. And, just as in a fairy tale, the enchanted palace had turned into a gloomy cave and her Prince Charming had turned into a frog.

Now, as she shut the oven door on their TV dinners, she slipped away from the crowding touch of his belly, avoiding his eyes, loathing his proximity. She now detested every sound, every odor, every touch and sight connected with Walter. She hated his slobbery snore, his guiltless belches and farts; she hated the bridge that he was always taking out and leaving in unexpected places, she hated his gap-toothed appearance without it; she hated the sour socks and stained undershorts that he never bothered to put in the hamper; she hated his infuriating, incurable habit of pissing on the toilet seat.

He set water to boil and took the coffee out of the refrigerator. He did it with slightly exaggerated care. In his maddening body language, that was meant as a rebuke to her for not having done it.

"I read in this marriage manual where more than sixty percent of married couples engage in – oral sex prior to intercourse," Walter said.

It took a moment for his words to sink in and, at first, she wasn't sure she'd heard him correctly above the sound of running water. He turned off the tap and stared at her. She pretended to ignore him.

"I read that in a medical book, you know, by a doctor," he said. "A fellow at the mill had it."

"Do you normally discuss our intimate relations with your employees at the mill, Walter?" she asked, facing him and injecting her voice with an arctic chill.

"No, of course not, we were talking about sex in general and he brought in this book. It was just one of your normal bull sessions, a couple of guys talking about stuff, you know."

"Yes, you were always a great one for those," she said; but again she knew that using sarcasm on Walter was like hitting one of those inflatable Bozos that can never be knocked down.

"What I meant was, since sixty percent of married people do it, I mean, modern couples and all, maybe it would be interesting if you would do it to me sometimes. Just to try it, like for – ah – variety, you know."

"Do what?"

"Blow me."

"Oh, Christ, you . . . you're impossible!" she snapped as she whirled and strode out of the kitchen.

She'd left because she hadn't known whether to scream at him or laugh at him. He was so damned inept, so clumsy. Maybe her best reaction would have been to call his bluff and agree to do it then and there. She thought of all the time and effort that she'd spent during their marriage prettying herself up, hinting that they ought to go to bed, trying to distract Walter's interest from some *film noir* classic on TV that he'd seen seventeen times before, or from the intricacies of the fifty-thousand-dollar toy train set in their basement. Having been distracted, he would trudge upstairs to brush his teeth and gargle lengthily, put his bridge to soak, spray his. armpits, don his pajamas, turn off the bedroom lights, and climb into bed. He would briefly subject her to some foreplay as stylized and predictable as the motions of a man buying a candy bar from a coin machine. Pushing his pajama-bottoms to his knees, he would mount her, enter her, achieve a gasping climax, roll away, pull up his pajamas and go to sleep.

So now, after seventeen years of dull, uninspired, face-to-face fucking, Walter had conceived the notion that he'd like to try a blowjob. Instead of mentioning it in the bedroom in the course of making love, he'd brought it up while she was trying to cook dinner and hurry out of the house. Worst of all, he'd *mentioned* it, in the silly jargon of a marriage manual.

She laughed aloud as she recalled that she had once seen Walter as a romantic alternative to her parents' prosaic drabness. It was partly to escape their narrow views, their petty rules and restrictions, that she'd married him. She'd thought that she was madly in love with him. Now, she knew, she'd been madly in love with the idea of striking out on her own, buying, furniture, making a home – in short, playing house with a man who was as docile and safe as her old teddy bear. During their courtship, his tentative fumblings and gropings had aroused her to feelings that she hadn't known about. She'd thought that he was opening a whole knew world to her. Only by slow degrees had she learned that he could only show her the door to that world, that he didn't possess the key.

Walter poked his head around the door of the kitchen like an immense groundhog fearful of seeing its shadow. "How about the TV dinners, hon?"

"Dear, would you take them out of the oven? I don't know if I'll even have time to eat mine. I'm not dressed yet."

"You got to eat, honey. Next thing you know, you'll be sick."

"I can grab a bite at Koerner's later."

"It's bad enough just going out in the street at night anymore, without you should go to Koerner's. It's full of niggers and hairy hippies these days."

He withdrew to the kitchen. She sighed. A few white youths with long hair and tattered denims, and some blacks who affected Afros and sunglasses and berets, gathered in front of Koerner's drugstore every night to horse around with each other and comment on the passersby. They were just boys, playing as boys have always played, but they scared Walter out of his wits. Forced to walk past them, he would lower his head and quicken his pace and hold his breath. His face would whiten around the lips.

Walter's imagination peopled the cricket-loud New England night with mobs of vengeful blacks, bomb-throwing radicals, and carloads of psychopathic thrill-killers. He owned a gun and he checked every one of the many locks at night. She had long ago given up trying to convince him that the first precaution was dangerous, the second probably useless.

"This is a man's job, Katy, protecting the home," he would say with sententious smugness. "You don't know about these things."

Maybe she was being too harsh. It was perhaps understandable that someone who had been beaten up regularly in a schoolyard for four years should grow up to regard the world as hostile and dangerous. No, damn it, she wasn't being harsh enough: a man, a real man, would have risen above those early cruelties. Walter, instead, had descended to his basement to build little towns without people, to run little trains without passengers.

She hurried to the bedroom to dress. She had outgrown Walter Burroughs. It had been an odd process, because she'd always associated growth with getting older, but she had grown by getting younger, or at least by watching Walter slide beyond her into the chasm of middle age. She felt younger now than when, as a frizzed-up moppet in garish lipstick, she'd stammered her way through the valedictory address at the Armitage High School gym.

She chose a yellow silk shift, floor length and slit up the side to the hip, and a colorful East Indian vest decorated with beads and bits of mirror. She ordered such clothes from New York boutiques, then could wear them only to places like the Library Society. She hoped Quentin would appreciate her sophistication. He was constantly impressing her with his, speaking casually of Yucatan or Ibiza in the manner of a man intimately familiar with such exotic places. Walter could have afforded to take her anywhere in the world, of course. They could have afforded to buy a home anywhere in the world, but he had to stay in Armitage and keep his trains running. "I can't take you to Paris, hon," she could imagine him saying, "I'll miss *Kiss of Death* on the late show."

Walter sat in the kitchen, picking carefully at the gray blob alleged to be sauerbraten so as not to pierce the tinfoil dish with his knife and fork.

"Gee, you look swell, hon," he said. "Really great."

The lamplight gleamed on the freckled scalp above his temples, emphasizing how much of his sparse hair he'd lost in just the past year. Maybe that came from wearing that stupid hat he wore when he played with his trains.

"You better sit down before it gets cold," he said.

"I can't really. I'm late already."

"I'm sorry I – well, you know, was so blunt, or whatever you call it, before, you know, when I said . . . It's just that . . ." His teddy-bear eyes were mournful.

"It's all right." She patted his huge, soft shoulder.

"We got to talk sometime, like we always used to – in the old days. Sometimes I think we were a hell of a lot better off when we lived –"

"Sure, we'll talk sometime. Enjoy your movie," she said as she hurried out the door.

"Be careful," he said, following her. "You know, they had on the network news tonight about that rapist. Some cop named LaPlante said how nobody in town was really safe."

"Piffle," Katy said.

"What?" She didn't repeat it.

Chapter Four

Frank Buchanan believed that he had seen everything, now that he had seen Ma Corcoran in a sheer black nightie. It was something he had never expected to see, like a shark in a bikini. Without thinking about it, he had always believed that her baggy Army fatigue pants and oversized plaid shirts were integral parts of her anatomy.

He found it hard to overcome the weirdness of the sight and concentrate on the substance of the interview. Her lean, leathery face with its thin lips and protuberant blue eyes; her Orphan Annie mop of dyed red curls; her calloused, oversized hands and feet: these looked like crudities that some prankster had pasted on a picture of a pinup girl.

It wasn't really a pinup girl's body, though; it was more like that of a competitive swimmer, chunky and solid. At any rate, it looked twenty years younger than the rest of her. He knew that she was somewhere in her forties. In her everyday clothes, she could have passed for sixty. But her breasts were as firm and high as a teenager's. They were a lot larger than he had supposed, too. It was difficult to keep his eyes off the big, dark badges of her nipples, clearly visible through the flimsy garment.

She saw the direction of his gaze and casually arranged to let the nightie gape a little wider. Below the sun-browned triangle at her throat, her skin was like cream.

"How come you didn't bring flowers?" she asked, talking around the Camel dangling from her lip. "You're a lousy excuse for a date."

He realized that his initial shock had put him at a disadvantage. "I came here on business, Ma," he said.

"What other kind of date is there?" She took the cigarette out and brayed in his face. Her bad teeth cancelled much of her appeal. "And don't call me *Ma.*" She added with monstrous coyness, "My name is Marjorie."

"Let's talk about Saturday night, Marjorie."

"Another date so soon? I'll have to check and see if I'm free." She crossed her legs, perhaps deliberately giving him a momentary glimpse of her dark-brown pubic bush.

He was able to ignore the display. "I'm talking about last Saturday night, when you were up at Sutton's Pond."

"Bullshit. I was home watching Mary Tyler Moore, my ideal, Ask Sonny."

"I'm not a game warden. You can fling around all the dynamite you want to outside city limits."

She crushed the beer can in her hand and let it drop to the floor. The outside of her two-story frame house was clean and recently painted. The lawn was as neat as an astronaut's crew cut. But inside, the house looked like a Woolworth store that had been struck by a tornado. A new color TV equipped with video recorder and camera was conspicuous in the cheap clutter.

"You want a beer?" she asked. She got up and picked

her way through the debris to the kitchen. Her nightie didn't cover her ass. It was a great ass, and her legs were long and shapely. Maybe he should try coming on with her. Ma wouldn't have admitted him to the house without a warrant unless she'd liked his looks.

"I'll take that beer, Marjorie, okay?"

He rejected his idea after a moment's thought. Maybe he could put a bag over her head, but he couldn't put one over his soul.

She came back with two beers. Her walk was normally as feminine as a paratrooper's, but now she transformed it. The delta of dark curls below the hem of her garment wigwagged at him as she swung her hips.

"Why should I trust you with anything?" she asked, handing him the beer. "Everybody says you're a son-of-a-bitch."

"Because I got no interest in anything you're doing; that's all I can tell you."

"Yeah, cop. And next week you might be interested. Drink your beer, and let's talk about your sexy green eyes."

"You're fond of Sonny, aren't you?"

Her face instantly lost its warmth. Her bulging blue eyes now held as little human sympathy as a snake's. It was a chilling performance. She would have made a good police interrogator.

"I mentioned him because those kids who were killed are even younger than he is. They have mothers, too. How do you suppose you'd feel if some nut burned him alive?"

Some of the chill left her eyes. She smiled slightly, perhaps thinking of what she'd do to such a person.

"I thought they were shot," she said at last.

"The shots didn't kill them."

"What a creep!" She shook her head and smiled at

her beer can.

"I won't tell you about your civic duty, because I know you think that's a lot of crap. But maybe your feelings as a mother would make you want to help."

Frank had never heard such bullshit in his life, but it seemed to be going over. Her moment of hostility had passed. She sighed, and her eyes once more seemed like those of a human being when she looked at him.

"Okay, I was up there. But I didn't hear anything. I didn't see anybody."

"What time did you set off the charge?

She scowled. "You want a lot for nothing, don't you? All right. Just after midnight. As you can imagine, I didn't stick around very long. Less than an hour. I came and went by the back way, I didn't go within a mile of the monument, but I would have heard shots. I didn't."

"You didn't hear any cars in the woods?"

"I told you, nothing. Did you ever get laid on satin sheets?"

"Yeah, we kept sliding off," Frank said, and that again provoked her bray. When she had finished, he said, "Was Sonny with you?"

Immediately, he got the same reaction as before. Perhaps he had some leverage after all.

"The reason I asked, maybe he heard or saw something you didn't."

"That'll be the day," she laughed. "No, I was alone."

He placed no special weight on his next question; he asked it merely from habit: "Where was he?"

"Why don't you go home and practice blowing your whistle? You don't look so good to me anymore."

Frank gave her his best smile, but her response was still cool. "Look, I don't know anything about it, but it seems to me that if you're going to dynamite a pond, you want to bring along as many people as you can to help scoop up the fish."

"You're right, you don't know anything about it. I don't just 'scoop them up,' I select the best ones. It's like shopping. The same way I go for men," she said; and, reaching for a cigarette, she managed to bare one of her breasts completely.

She studied him through the smoke, not bothering to cover herself. Again he was struck by the ludicrous idea of a cartoon head on a voluptuous body.

"Do I have to talk to him and ask him where he was?"

His question produced the desired result: she jerked the nightie back across her naked breast.

"He was here. Watching TV with his girl."

"I didn't think he had one."

"You must not have been reading all the gossip columns. Gretchen Slovik."

Frank couldn't help laughing, but he was surprised when Ma Corcoran joined him with her jackass yawp. Gretchen Slovik was an amateur whore who hung out with Ma, who was probably trying to coach her up to a professional level. Ma had once run a whorehouse, but it went out of business when her two daughters ran away from home.

"Isn't he a little young for her?"

"That's a dumb question. He keeps her happy. He's got the biggest prick I ever saw, which is saying quite a lot." Raising an eyebrow, she stared speculatively at his crotch.

"Shopping for fish like that," he said, ignoring her stare, "it would be helpful to have a full moon, wouldn't it?"

"There was one."

"What I'm driving at, you had reasons to be up in the mountains on the nights of the full moon, when the rapist was up there. Maybe you saw something –"

"I can only dynamite the pond once a year. Christ,

I can't believe I'm sitting here telling all this to a cop. It must be love. Let's go and fuck."

"What about jacking deer?"

"Fucking is a lot more fun," she said, spreading her muscular thighs brazenly before him.

He had to admit she was getting to him. Even her face was beginning to look better.

"When you go out to shoot deer, don't you generally do it when you can see what you're doing? When there's a full moon?"

"I read the papers. I know when the girls got raped, and when I was in the woods. If I knew anything, I'd tell you. By the way, are you queer?"

"Think about it, Ma – Marjorie. There must have been other rapes that weren't reported. Maybe he's been doing this for years. Maybe you saw something odd on one of the nights he didn't make the papers."

"You're about the oddest thing I've seen," she said, recrossing her legs primly.

"What about Sonny? Does he go with you when you jack deer?"

"Hell, no. He doesn't believe in hurting animals."

"Just in beating the shit out of people, huh?"

"That was typical cop chickenshit. It was a fair fight, a private matter, until you cops stuck your noses into it."

She seemed filled with righteous anger now, and Frank laughed at her. Sonny was the self-appointed mayor of Division Street. He rousted drunks, interrogated strangers, broke up noisy parties; he would remonstrate with householders for not mowing their lawns, or for watering them during proscribed hours; he had charge of the sawhorses that were used to close off a block as a play-street after school hours; although he was only eighteen and unmarried, he was the organizer and chairman of the Block Parents in his neighborhood. Sometimes he flashed a mail-order badge to legitimize his authority. It was an odd reversal of roles: the son was the neighborhood busybody, and the mother acted like a juvenile delinquent.

Sonny stood six-foot-six and had nothing but muscles on his gangling bones. He was pale as death and always wore black sunglasses. He looked like a skeleton that had taken up weightlifting. Sometimes he would scare the hell out of people, and they would go to the police, who tried to mollify them. The police took a benign attitude toward Sonny, even winking at his badge-flashing; they, regarded him as a harmless crackpot who saved them a lot of work.

Sonny had a juvenile record composed chiefly of assaults that, in an adult, would have been classified as attempted murder. In one instance, at the age of fourteen, he had run over one of Ma's boyfriends with a car – six times – necessitating the amputation of both the man's legs.

But Sonny had reformed, or so everyone had thought, and he had reformed in an odd way: his contact with the police had turned him into a police buff. When he wasn't managing things on Division Street, he hung out at police headquarters, his presence tolerated in return for errands like going for coffee and sandwiches. It was his burning ambition to become a policeman, but he didn't stand a chance. Intelligence tests classified him as "dull normal," and he could barely read or write. He had flunked the simple written test for patrolman four times. Compared to Sonny Corcoran, Ronnie Elkins was the glorious crown and culmination of human intellectual evolution.

One of Sonny's projects was a series of flowerbeds in the island that ran down the middle of Division Street. He obtained seeds and fertilizer from the City Council, turned the earth, planted the flowers, and maintained them with loving industry. He was given a write-up with his picture in the *Advertiser,* and the Junior Chamber of Commerce made him their Man of the Year.

There lived on Division Street a man named Jackson, who had a dog named Sparky. Jackson ignored the city's leash-law and let Sparky run loose late at night. Set free, Sparky would head straight for Sonny's flowerbeds to relieve himself. Sonny, who would set his alarm clock for odd hours of the night so he could go out and patrol the street, observed this. He tracked the dog home and expostulated with Jackson, who told him to go fuck himself. Sonny went and got his baseball bat and put Jackson in the hospital for six months.

Despite his record, Sonny's impressive array of character witnesses – policemen, JayCees, even the chairperson of the City Beautification Commission – drew him a suspended sentence. He was now on probation.

That was why Frank had laughed at Ma Corcoran's indignation: in his view, Sonny was a homicidal moron who would one day run across his fated victim.

"What's he doing now, Ma?"

Sitting stiffly, she didn't acknowledge his lapse from "Marjorie." She crumpled her beer can and let it drop. Frank took the second sip from his.

"Why don't you ask his probation officer," she said, heaving herself out of the chair and trudging to the kitchen with no attempt to modify her normal paratrooper walk. Nevertheless, she still had a great ass.

He followed her to the kitchen. A shiny-new freezer of impressive capacity – full of dynamited trout and illegal deer – looked incongruous amid the footworn linoleum, the stained sink, the grease-browned walls. A hole in the ceiling revealed rusty pipes. He also noted a new microwave oven and a Cuisinart. He supposed that Miss Slovik had lost her amateur status.

"Pretty fancy," he said.

"I don't know why I let you in," she said, popping the flip-top of a fresh can. "You looked like a nice guy, a guy who might be good for some laughs, but you're just another prick cop. You'd think I'd know better by now. That's always been my major fault, expecting good things from men. I guess I saw too many John Wayne movies when I was a kid. Tell me, cop, in all your years as a bully and a head-beater, have you ever run across a woman who would do something like burn a couple of kids alive in the trunk of a car?"

"Women have their own faults."

"They ought to have Paul Newman or Robert Redford play a part like that, where they rape and torture and murder. Maybe it would set the record straight. How's your beer?"

"Just fine."

"Christ, you're a bastard. You pretend to drink with me and be my pal, and you just lap around the edges like a pussycat. Pussycat eyes. And you don't even make a sound when you walk. Did anybody ever tell you that, pussycat?"

She flung herself against him and raised her face, eyes closed, to be kissed. Her moving thigh touched the evidence of his interest.

"So what's Sonny doing now, Ma?" he asked.

"Oh, shit." She pushed herself away from him. Her beer was empty, and, she opened another. "He's got a great job at the Burroughs Thread Mill. It's the same one Walter Burroughs started with, and look where he wound up." She laughed, but her laughter fell short of her hearty bray.

"Where's his room?"

She stared hard at him for a moment. "You no longer amuse me, cop. Get the fuck out of my house!"

Frank shrugged. "Okay. Maybe I'll talk to Sonny and

ask him a couple of questions. Maybe he won't like my questions and he'll get mad. Maybe I'll push him a little, and he'll get violent." He drew the .357 Magnum Colt Python from his shoulder holster and popped out the cylinder to examine the rounds. He snapped it shut and reholstered it. "Maybe you better show me his room."

For an instant he thought that he might have overplayed his hand. Hatred blazed in her eyes; and, even worse, intelligence. She could have stood on her rights and thrown him out. She could have called a lawyer, or even police headquarters, and gotten him into deep trouble for running his own, unsanctioned investigation. But she knew his reputation; and, like most criminals would, she assumed that at least half his killings had been setups, that he'd planted weapons on their bodies after execution. Sonny, and the cynicism rooted in her own immorality, were her two weak points.

She gestured, but he waited for her to lead him. She went back to the living room and up the stairs. He followed, annoyed with himself for still finding her exciting. From the back, her cunt looked like a ripe, cleft peach beneath her strong buttocks. He would have liked to make her gibber with pleasure while he stood, apart in some cold place in his mind and watched her writhe, asserting his power over her.

He entered Sonny's room after her. It was far neater and cleaner than any room he had seen in the house. The iron-framed cot was made up with neat hospital corners. The bureau and desk were free of litter and dust. On the walls hung framed photographs of wild animals and framed copies of newspaper stories about Sonny's attempts at civic improvement. His library included comic books, muscle magazines, jerk-off books, *The Road to Oz,* a Bible, a Boy Scout handbook.

The closet held barbells, one dark blue suit, a winter coat, several pairs of jeans, and a shoebox full of newspaper clippings about Walter Burroughs and his company.

Frank couldn't say when the possibility had first struck him, but it fascinated him: that Sonny Corcoran was the Full Moon Maniac. He had a history of near-murderous violence. He was an oddball. The attitude toward women that he had derived from childhood experiences must have been nightmarish. Like all descriptions of the Maniac, he was very large. Best of all, his mother was in the habit of roaming the hills at night. Regardless of what she'd said, she probably took him along on her excursions. While she poached deer, she told him to run along and amuse himself: which he did by raping and murdering.

The Maniac was in the habit of taking souvenirs. A shoe from one victim, a pair of panties from another. Melody Boisvert had always worn a bra, her mother said, but it hadn't been found. If he found it here – well, if he found it here he would have to figure out a way of getting around the rules against unlawful search and seizure, but he had done so in the past.

"Does he have a gun?" he asked.

"He's on probation," Ma said. "Any guns you find in this house are mine."

He smiled as he rummaged through the drawers of the bureau. Ma had shot her first husband in self-defense, a jury had decided, and her second in a hunting accident. He went on to check the desk, where Sonny had neatly filed all his junk mail, probably the only correspondence be ever received. He discovered nothing except the fact that Sonny wasn't a slob like his mother. He must have learned neatness in reform school.

Frank would have liked to take the room apart, but

he couldn't have justified that in a court; and Ma was getting impatient. She leaned in the doorway, smoking and dropping the ashes on Sonny's clean rug. The only reason she could have had for permitting this search was her absolute certainty that her son had nothing to hide, but Frank wasn't ready to buy that. Not even Sonny Corcoran, he was sure, told his mother everything.

"He's a good kid, cop, he's straight as an arrow," she said, adding thoughtfully: "Sometimes I wonder if they didn't make a mistake at the hospital. His father was an even worse prick than you are."

Totally disillusioned with him, Ma tried no more of her seductive wiles as he left the house, and Frank was grateful for that. He was so horny now that he probably would have said to hell with it and succumbed. He planned to call up Angelique when he finished for the night. Her doughy body wasn't as good as Ma's, but he would be able to face himself in the mirror tomorrow.

Instead of going to his car, he walked back into the Corcorans' driveway. Ma's beat-up Land Rover was parked in the drive. He tried the doors, but they were locked. He went on to the garage, which was also locked. He saw a car through the dirty window of the garage. He took out the pencil-flash on his key-ring and shone it through the window. He saw a white Pinto, apparently brand new. He was unable to see the license plate.

He walked back down the drive. Ma hadn't gotten rich from ether of her husbands, and she had no job. The small-time fencing and procuring that she did provided her with little more than beer and cigarette money. She did her poaching mostly for fun, but partly because it was the only way to beat the supermarkets. In the fall and winter, she and Sonny would take a chainsaw into the woods and haul back firewood to sell. The proceeds from that were probably eaten up by taxes on her house and by utility bills. Gretchen Slovik certainly hadn't brought in seven or eight thousand dollars in the past couple of months, but that was the approximate value of Ma's shiny new toys.

The likeliest explanation seemed to be that Ma's two-bit fencing had gotten her a connection with a high-powered operation: either a bigger fence, or else a gang of warehouse thieves or hijackers. He was annoyed with himself for not having thought to note the serial numbers of the new appliances in her kitchen. He doubted that she would ever let him through the door again.

He got into his fire-engine red Mustang convertible, a relic that he couldn't bring himself to part with, and let down the top. He didn't know what he'd do when this car died on him, as it was constantly threatening to do. Nobody made convertibles anymore.

He owed Ronnie Elkins a debt of gratitude. Ronnie had diligently questioned all the bystanders early Sunday morning. Confused as always, he had made his report on Monday to Frank instead of Capt. LaPlante. He hadn't found anyone who had heard shots. Even the warden who had reported the fire had been too far away. But he did find someone who lived a half-mile from Sutton's Pond who had heard a curious noise like a muffled explosion around midnight. Guessing the truth already, Frank called the local fish and game warden, who told him that all the fish in Sutton's Pond had been found floating belly up on Sunday morning. He didn't need to tell Frank whom he suspected of having done what.

He supposed he could repay his debt to Bonnie by redirecting him to Capt. LaPlante with his information, but that would only be asking for trouble.

LaPlante would come to the same conclusion he had, go to Ma Corcoran, and discover that she'd already been questioned by a detective assigned to another case. The captain's thorough, plodding legwork would eventually turn up the witness who had heard the explosion, but anything could have happened by then. Maybe Frank would have succeeded in shaking something loose from Sonny Corcoran, or from his alibi, Gretchen Slovik.

He toured the town aimlessly, not deliberately searching for Sonny or Gretchen. His drive took him past the thread mill. Sonny's box of clippings about Walter Burroughs and the mill seemed another example of his compulsive behavior. Now that he was no longer encouraged to hang around police headquarters and had gotten a job at the mill, he had apparently become a thread-mill buff.

He spotted Sonny ambling down Main Street, towering over the passersby. He parked by the, nearest hydrant and got out without raising the top. He tailed Sonny.

Tailing Sonny was unexpectedly difficult. He recrossed the street at least four times. He kept bending to fuss with the laces of his tennis shoes, paused to browse in unlikely store windows. Once he did an abrupt about-face that caught Frank completely off guard. He thought for a moment that Sonny had made him, but apparently not: he hadn't even seen him through those opaque sunglasses. But Sonny acted like a man who was expecting to spot a tail.

When Sonny halted unexpectedly to check out the fixtures in the window of Murchison's Plumbing Supply Co., Frank at last figured out what was going on. Sonny was tailing somebody. He was following a dark-haired woman in a yellow dress who had stopped for a moment to gaze into the window of Koerner's Drugstore.

Chapter Five

Katy couldn't recall when she had ever been so oppressed by the dullness of Armitage. The boxlike regularity of Main Street, roofed from the sky by the glare of mercury vapor lamps, made her want to scream. Even the traffic light at the corner of Broad Street offended her. It changed from green to orange to red with mechanistic idiocy, even though there was barely any traffic to control in the middle of town at this hour. She had thought that walking to the library instead of driving would lift her mood, but it seemed to have accomplished just the opposite.

A few teenage loafers were silhouetted by the fluorescent plate glass of Koerner's Drugstore. Defying Walter's nightmares, she walked right up to them to look in the window.

Without a word, they stepped politely aside and ignored her to continue a conversation about the Boston Red Sox. So much for Walter's dope-crazed juvenile delinquents.

She recalled that the drugstore window had been a source of fascination to her as a child. Dusty and cluttered and dark, it had been filled with fancifully shaped bottles full of brightly colored fluids. She had imagined them to be magical potions like those that Alice drank in Wonderland. They were only colored water, her mother had explained, with the flat, matter-of-fact bluntness she used for smashing Katy's dreams. Now the small-paned display window had been replaced by a sheet of plate glass, glaringly lighted, and the bottles were long gone.

Her mother had approved wholeheartedly of Walter. But the vivid hues of his sensitivity and earnestness and warmth had turned out to be only colored water, too.

She approached Elm Street, where the library was located, where Quentin Swift waited for her. She remembered a Christmas season – perhaps she'd been twelve – when she'd walked downtown with her father to do some last-minute shopping. Stars had trembled in a sky of blue-black crystal, and each breath she took brought with it the special little bite that comes with subzero air. Walking down Elm Street, they heard singing in a bright house. They stopped to listen to a tenor and a small chorus singing "O Holy Night." She'd never heard anything so beautiful. Standing in a deep trench between mountains of shoveled snow, her mittened hand engulfed by her father's, she was filled with wonder and warmth and expectancy. That was what life ought to be like all the time, but she had never recaptured the precise blend of emotions, not even at Christmas when she'd heard the same carol. She certainly felt nothing like it at the prospect of meeting Quentin. If only she could find someone really new, really different!

"Lady?"

The voice at her elbow made her jump. She had turned into the wooded gloom of Elm Street. She saw a giant figure in white who stared down at her with black sockets for eyes – no, no, of course not, they were sunglasses. She began breathing again.

"I'm sorry I scared you," he said. His deep, sepulchral voice kept up the illusion that he was a black-and-white image that had just wandered off the screen of an old horror film.

The main street wasn't far, and there were lights in all the surrounding houses. She was angry with herself for reacting just as Walter would have. She smiled at him and said, "What do you want?"

"I want to talk to you. You're Mrs. Burroughs," he stated.

"'By thy long gray beard and glittering eye, now wherefore stop'st thou me?'" she quoted, gaily, she had hoped, but it came out sounding a shade hysterical.

"Huh?"

"It's a poem," she said. "About someone who pops up out of the darkness with a story to tell."

"I don't know much about poems," he said.

"Well, why don't you come along to the library with me while we talk? I'll show you the poem."

"I want to talk to you," he repeated. "It's kind of important. A personal matter."

"Well, start," she said, walking on. "Why don't you start with your name?"

"It's Raymond," he said, trying to adapt his huge stride to her pace. "Raymond Corcoran."

"Well, my name is Katy, Raymond. I'm glad to meet you."

"I work for your husband."

She shot him a quick look. The phrase was one that an executive would have used, but he didn't look to her like executive material. He was far too muscular for an office-bound man, too. It took her a moment to realize he only meant that he worked at the mill, and she chided herself for snobbery.

"What do you do for him?"

"I got the same job he used to have," he said. "Ma always says, 'Look where he wound up,' but she's just making a joke." He laughed. His laughter sounded like something he had seen demonstrated on television, but which he hadn't quite gotten the knack of doing himself. Katy joined him uneasily.

"I think he's a great man," Raymond said.

"He'd be pleased to hear that."

"Oh, he must know it. Running that big business and all, that takes real brains. You got to know how to tell people what to do, and make it stick. That's not easy, I know. I tell them the right thing they ought to do, and they just go and do something else, like little kids. Sometimes it makes me so mad I want to smash them, them going and doing what's wrong when they know it's wrong. Only Mr. Burroughs just tells people what to do and they do it, and he don't – *doesn't* have to smash anybody."

At first she had thought with dismay that Raymond was an employee with a grievance, that he would burden her with some involved complaint that she didn't want to know about. She had thought that his praise of Walter was ironic. Walter, after all, knew as little about the business as she did, even though he made a show of going to his office for a few hours a day to be "briefed" by the hired hands who ran it for him. But Raymond wasn't being ironic. He was a fan of Walter's. It was all she could do to keep a straight face.

"I read about him in the papers all the time," Raymond said. "Like when he spoke to the Rotary Club on April 15, 1976, and said, 'Nowhere in all the world, nowhere in all of history, has a government-regulated economy produced such prosperity for the workers as under our own time-tested free-market system.'"

This was wonderful! This was priceless! She had to

take this nonpareil into the Library Society and introduce him to some of the people who knew Walter. She would have to introduce him to Walter, for that matter. And she'd been thinking that life in Armitage was dull!

"Some of the things he says are even better than poems, when you think about them," Raymond said. "I'm not a very fast reader, and I have to look up a lot of his words in the dictionary, but that makes me think about them harder and understand how important and right they are."

Maybe she should introduce him to Jay Rosenstein, too; he was the vice president in charge of public relations who wrote Walter's speeches.

"I read in the paper where he has a railroad layout that he built all by himself, with little towns and factories and everything. That takes brains, too; those kits can be very complicated, and they always put something in the instructions that turns out to be not right. Only I can't afford to build a model railroad; I went to the hobby store and found that much out." He brooded silently for a moment, then added: "I was building this model airplane once that was real hard; it was the hardest thing I ever did. I was doing it right, too. Just when I got all the hard parts done, Ma stepped on it in the dark."

"I'm sorry," Katy said.

"She was drunk. Sometimes she does real nasty things when she's drunk, I mean nasty things I couldn't tell you about, but that was just an accident. I wanted to smash her, but I didn't."

"Here we are," she said. "Come on in."

"No, I don't want to go in there. I never been in there."

"That's all the more reason," she said, taking his arm; and shocked by the feel of it. Compared to Walter's flesh or Quentin's, or that of any other man she'd ever touched, it was like something made of iron. She felt an indefinable little throb that wasn't exactly desire: it was more like curiosity. "That's all the more reason," she repeated. "If you like to read, and you so obviously do, then this is a place you should have discovered long ago. Professor Swift, a very intelligent man – smarter even than Walter, believe it or not – is going to talk about some books that you'd probably like. They're like fairy tales, only –"

"How do you know I like fairy tales?" he demanded.

"Well, I don't know, you seem so –" She hesitated. "Simple" was the first word that came to mind, in its good sense, and "childlike" was the second, but she suspected that he might misconstrue her meaning. She finished lamely, "– so much like somebody who would like them. I like them, too."

"Well, I don't want to hear about them. Nobody is smarter than Mr. Burroughs, either; that's a dumb thing to say."

"Well, I have to go in. It was nice talking to you, Raymond," she said, turning to leave, but he gripped her arm.

"I told you, I got to talk to you about something important."

"You mean, all that wasn't it?"

He shook his head. "Of course not. This is personal, and it's very hard to talk about, and it'll take a long time."

She wavered. Quentin would natter on about Tolkien for at least an hour, with a discussion period afterward; and Raymond's story certainly wouldn't take that long. And she believed that nothing Quentin could possibly say about Tolkien would have the interest of whatever this original might come up with.

They stood under a streetlight, and its glare seemed to bother him. Still gripping her arm firmly in his huge, knobby hand, he gazed up and down the street.

"Let's go across to the park and sit down," he said at last.

"I don't know whether I can trust you," she said, trying hard not to make it sound coy, but not succeeding.

"You mean you think I won't tell you the truth? I never tell lies."

"No, that isn't what I meant. What I mean is, it's dark over there, and you're so big and strong, and –"

"You think I'd make you do nasty things?" he asked, shocked, even horrified. "You're Mr. Burroughs's wife, I'd *never* do nasty things with you!"

Shit, Katy thought, surprising herself.

"All right," she said. "You said you never tell lies, so I guess I have to believe you."

Raymond released her, but she slipped her hand through his arm as they crossed the street. He acted as if he had never walked with a woman on his arm before.

"When you talk about 'nasty things,'" she said, "do you mean sex?"

"Yeah," he grunted.

"That isn't a very healthy attitude," she said as they passed into the darkness of the park. "Sex isn't nasty at all." She thought about Walter, pumping between her legs with boring automatism. "At least, it doesn't have to be. Why do you think sex is nasty?"

He was silent for a while, and she congratulated herself on her intelligence, her broad-mindedness, her courage. Walter was a complete fool. People were basically good. You just needed the courage to respond to them, the intelligence to draw them out, the broad-mindedness to understand them. By simply accepting a stranger as a friend, she had unexpectedly found herself in a fascinating discussion.

"I guess it's not sex that's nasty, it's Gretchen," he

said. "When I touch her, you know, between her legs, my hand smells like old sardines."

She tried not to laugh. "Is Gretchen your girl?"

"Of course not! That's what Ma says, though, to get me mad. Were you talking to Ma?"

"No, I haven't even met her. Who's Gretchen?"

They had reached the edge of the pond, where a few lights illuminated the path at its side. They walked to a bench and sat down.

"Gretchen's just a friend of Ma's. Ma likes to watch me do things to her."

"What do you mean? Do what to her?"

"You know, what we were talking about. Sex."

Katy stared at him, but it was impossible to read his expression behind those dark glasses. She was beginning to suspect that she was being made the butt of an elaborate practical joke, perhaps cooked up by Quentin Swift and some gifted drama student from the state university. She couldn't quite believe it, though. No drama student could possibly be this good.

"Let me get this straight," she said. "When you say 'Ma,' you're talking about your mother, right? Your real mother?"

"Yeah, of course."

"And she makes you screw this friend of hers so she – your mother – can watch?"

"Yeah, only that's not the kind of word you ought to use."

"That's *horrible!* I never heard of anything like that! Why do you let them do it?"

"Well, it's not like I let them. I want to do it, when Gretchen starts fooling around with me and taking off her clothes. I don't really mind so much, and Gretchen doesn't mind at all, and Ma likes to watch. It would be better if it wasn't somebody fat and smelly, like Gretchen."

"Jesus Christ. You aren't pulling my leg, are you?"

"I wouldn't do that. Ask Ma."

"No, thank you. If you want my advice, you ought to get away from that mother of yours and find yourself a nice girl."

"Ma isn't so bad. Sometimes we have a lot of fun together, like when we go out and hunt. I don't like to kill animals, but it's fun to be out in the woods with Ma; she's like another guy. But she's had a lot of trouble with her dumb boyfriends and all, so she drinks too much, and she gets funny when she drinks."

"I bet she does."

"Anyway, I never met no – *any* – nice girls."

"Thanks a lot, buddy! What am I supposed to be?"

"I didn't mean you! A man like Mr. Burroughs wouldn't have a wife who wasn't nice."

She couldn't help adding: "I don't smell like sardines, either."

He looked away, confused and embarrassed.

She began to understand why some men are fascinated by the proverbial dumb bunny. It was exhilarating to know and feel herself so totally superior to a member of the opposite sex, to be able to tease him and manipulate him the way a matador does a bull, to guide him the way a trainer guides a huge, dull elephant. She was totally superior to Walter, of course, but that was entirely different. His inferiority derived from a sour smallness of soul, while Raymond's stemmed from simple, charming stupidity.

She couldn't deny, either, that an electric little thrill had been mingled with her revulsion at his description of his home life. People might deplore the morals of Erskine Caldwell's characters, but they loved to read about them. She bad pictured the scene – the drunken mother, the fat and smelly friend, the simpleminded son – in far more detail than he had described it, and it had aroused her. The thought of going back to the library and implementing her plan for Quentin Swift was unappetizing. She sensed a possibility for adventure and excitement here that she had never even dreamed of before. She wondered what it would be like to make love among the bushes of a public park.

"Want to find out?" she asked.

"Huh?"

"I said, do you want to find out?"

"Find out what?"

She moistened her lips with her tongue. "Whether I smell like Gretchen."

He jerked away, putting a foot of space between them on the bench. "Don't make fun of me. I don't like it."

She inched toward him. "I'm not making fun of you, honest. I like you, I really do. I wouldn't come out here in the park to make fun of you, would I?"

The black glasses faced her, but she had no idea what he might be thinking. Never having seduced anyone before, she was at a loss about what to do next. She recalled his saying that Gretchen aroused him by taking off her clothes. Thinking about it wouldn't get it done. She made a conscious effort to switch off her mind. With a quick, jerky motion she pulled her skirt up. She pushed her black panties down and freed her legs from them. Christ, what was she doing!

"Aren't I nicer than Gretchen?"

"You're as bad as she is. You're worse than she is. You're married to Mr. Burroughs," he said angrily.

"Raymond, I hate to disillusion you," she said, reaching back to undo the buttons at her neck, "but Mr. Burroughs is a twerp. An asshole. A zero."

"Don't say that," he growled. "Don't you ever say that to me."

"All right, Raymond, let's forget about him, then. People tell me I'm pretty. Don't you think I am?" She wriggled the dress over her head and threw it aside.

"You're beautiful," he said with feeling; then added, "but you're not very nice."

She was beginning to regret her actions bitterly, but she couldn't back down, not now. She stood up in front of him, hipshot, and unbound her long, black hair.

"Come on, Raymond, what are you afraid of? I told you, sex isn't nasty. Let's do it, what do you say?"

She reached out to stroke his hair, and he batted her hand away with a stinging blow.

"Put your clothes on, you dirty whore. Put them on this minute, or I'll tell Mr. Burroughs on you. I'll tell!"

"Listen to me, Raymond. I'm not a whore, dirty or otherwise. My husband was the first and only man who's ever touched me. You're the only person besides him that I ever asked to do this, because I like you, because I think you're really nice and special," she said, but those words were no longer true: she would have liked, at this moment, to wring his stupid neck. "And if you're holding back because you admire my husband, you're – well, no, I won't say you're crazy. Your admiration is misplaced. He's a dull, stupid, narrow little man who'd probably be better off with Gretchen –"

Raymond stood up and she sat down. She couldn't understand why she had sat down so abruptly on the wet grass until, a moment later, the pain hit her. She raised her hand to her ear and screamed.

"You bitch, you dirty cunt!" Raymond shouted, standing over her like a tower. He fell on her and gripped her throat in his hands. "I hate you! I'm going to smash you! You're talking about my father!"

"You are crazy!" she wanted to scream, but all she could do was make croaking sounds as he buried his thumbs in her larynx. He crawled forward, dragging her beneath him. The water of the pond soaked her hair; its coolness touched her scalp. It stung her eyes, and the sky vanished.

Raymond released her neck. She pulled her head out of the water and struggled to sit up. He stood astride her legs with his back toward her. His shoulders heaved as if he were sobbing. He staggered. She imagined that he had regretted his act and was going through some terrible inner struggle to regain control.

"Raymond . . ."

His knees sagged and he doubled over, allowing her to see, for the first time, the man who was beating him as she'd never seen a fellow creature beaten before. He was hitting him with a little leather club on a spring handle, and it took her a moment to realize that it was blackjack, something she had only read of in novels about gangsters. He hit Raymond on the back of the neck, and Raymond collapsed to his hands and knees.

He crawled toward the man, who was certainly dressed flashily enough to be a gangster. His expression was chillingly aloof and uninvolved: he looked more like a doctor performing some complicated operation that he had done many times before than like a sadist administering a merciless beating: He fell on Raymond. His knee landed first, bearing all his weight, in the small of Raymond's back. Raymond screamed and lay thrashing on the ground as the man got up and studied him as if he were debating what atrocity to perpetrate next.

She stumbled to her feet and got between them, holding the man's arm and trying to push him back, but it was like trying to push back a brick wall.

"Stop it, stop it!" she cried. "Haven't you done enough to him?"

"Not nearly," he said quietly. His cool eyes made a leisurely tour of her body, and she was acutely embarrassed to remember her nakedness.

". . . kill you, Filthy Frank, you fucker," Raymond mumbled behind her.

"Excuse me," the red-haired man said with sardonic politeness as he pushed her to one side.

Raymond was trying to get up. He raised his face, swollen and bloody, and the man kicked it. He went down again, and the man kicked him in the stomach. Raymond writhed and twisted like a slug on a burning log.

"Stop it!" Katy screamed as loudly as she could. Her eye fell on the heavy leather, bag she had left on the park bench. She swung it with all her strength at the man's head, but he fended off the blow, laughing. "Police!" she shrieked. "Help, police!"

"I'm a police officer," he said. "As soon as I finish subduing this scumbag, I'll show you my badge. But please try to remember that I just saved your life, stupid."

When Raymond recovered himself enough to crawl this time, he crawled away. The "police officer" followed him without haste, like a confident cat following a mangled bird. She ran after him and grabbed his arm again.

"Please, please let him go! He didn't mean to hurt me. It was all my fault. I teased him, and –"

"I know," he interrupted. "Sonny is a very moral person. I think he raped and killed those kids the other night because he's opposed to fornication. When you wiggled your snatch at him, he figured you were a bad lady who ought to be punished."

Her cheeks burned. "No, I – I meant I teased him about my husband, I . . ."

Panic shut her up. Suppose he really was a policeman? She couldn't possibly tell him who she was, who her husband was. The scandal. Naked in the park with some half-wit she'd picked up on the street . . .

"I know who you are, Mrs. Burroughs," he said, smiling down at her, seeming to read her mind.

"But – you aren't going to make any charges, I mean –"

"Against him, or against you?" He laughed. "I got here in time for the show." He turned from her and shouted, "Good night, Sonny. I'll be talking to you."

"Don't you call me 'Sonny,' you prick!"

The man took a threatening step after him, and Raymond lurched into a shambling run. Katy seized the opportunity to run to her dress and pick it up. She was trying to untangle it when the man came up behind her. He slipped his arm around her waist and drew her into the darkness of the shrubbery behind the bench.

"Wait a minute!" she cried, trying to pull away from his firm grip. "What the hell is this? What do you think you're trying to do?"

"I wouldn't want you to go home disappointed. I feel sort of an obligation to you for chasing your boyfriend like that."

She had just opened her mouth to protest when he jammed his lips against hers and enfolded her in his arms. She struggled, but even she found her struggles unconvincing, and he just ignored them. Nothing that had happened to her had succeeded in cooling her need. It had merely been simmering, unnoticed, and this man – Christ, she didn't even know his *name!* – had effortlessly brought it back to a full boil.

She slid down in his arms and lay back on the damp grass. He stood over her, unbuckling his belt. In the middle of undressing, he hesitated. It struck her that he was worried about wrinkling his modish attire, that he was looking for a place to hang his trousers. She laughed at him. He laughed, too, and flung them aside.

Chapter Six

It was one of the biggest steam locomotives ever made, a monster with twelve driving wheels. It had been designed for the C&O to haul twisting dragons of coal cars out of the up-again-down-again wilderness of Appalachia. It slowed to a crawl on the long grade, hugging the pine-crested shoulder of a hill as it powered its way upward to yet another mine siding.

It was black with dirt and ash and soot, and its cavernous firebox was baked with rust. Only a sharp eye could have detected, under the accumulated grime of long; hard years of service, the emblem not of the C&O, but of the Armitage and Aylesbury Railroad. An expert in such trivia would also have noted that the design of the feedwater heater and the placement of the headlight distinguished it from a C&O engine.

Watching it worm forward with the inevitability of oncoming night, Walter Burroughs could almost hear its thunderous coughs and snorts racketing against the bones of the hills and hear the ululating echoes of its whistle. Almost: and that was testimony to his long hours of meticulous labor, because the hills were made of *papier-mâché* and the engine, less than sixteen inches in length, was a sculpture of lost-wax castings and tissue-thin brass sheeting. It drew a couple of amps of electricity for its power, and the only noise it ever really made was a buzz.

When new, the engine had gleamed like a piece of expensive jewelry, and every bolt and rivet had been modeled as close to the C&O prototype as Japanese craftsmen could make them. He'd needed guts to disassemble the shining engine, paint it to look as if it had seen years of rough use in the mountains, and put it back together again. His natural talents lay in the construction of scenery and miniature buildings. His father had always told him he'd had no mechanical aptitude whatever, and he'd never had reason to doubt that judgment. It was probably the most difficult challenge he'd ever accepted, but he'd taken the engine apart and put it back together; and when he was finished, it still worked.

He'd taken it apart many times since then, adding new refinements of filthiness or changing its profile to render it more clearly recognizable as an engine of the imaginary A&A. Most recently, he'd stripped it down to tinker with its electric motor and grind its gears to a more exact union with jeweler's rouge.

To Walter, the improvement he'd made with that last overhaul was dramatic. All suggestion of toy-train jerkiness had vanished. The engine crawled steadily, powerfully, as potently as if its weight were measured in tons rather than in ounces. His hand touched the throttle on his elaborate control board and the train slowed even further, grinding its immense mass up scale-miles of mountain gradient.

The only false note was in the payload: three cars, where the original might have hauled a hundred. But the tractive power of tiny models has its limits. He had a dream of some day stepping up to O-gauge. The larger scale made for much more power and realism. But their greater size would have necessitated buying a separate building; or maybe even having one constructed, and Katy would go through the roof if he even suggested such an expenditure. She didn't sympathize with his hobby at all. "It's so nice and neat, Walter," she would say on seeing a new model in the early stages of assembly. "Why do you have to go and deliberately make it look cruddy? I never heard of such an incredible case of misapplied talent."

There was an unused storage building at the mill on which he had long been casting a wistful eye. It had several thousand square feet of empty floor space and plenty of electrical outlets. He had even drawn up a tentative diagram of the dream layout in O-gauge that he would build there. But he knew that he would never work up the courage to do it. His employees laughed at him enough as it was. He scrupulously avoided the yard when the workers were coming or going, because someone would invariably make a "toot-toot" noise in the crowd behind his back.

He leaned closer to the tracks – tracks that had been hand laid with Lilliputian railroad spikes on individually scarred and weathered ties – to watch his favorite caboose go clicking by. Its apple-red hue was faded, and concealed in places by a dusting of soot and a spattering of mud. The old-fashioned tie-rods and trucks seemed scaly with rust, the result of an inspired paint job. The A&A sunburst was clearer than the one on the engine. Like that one, it was a decal printed to his design by a commercial supplier.

The caboose was basically a wooden kit, its parts razored and filed by Walter to tolerances that would have driven a watchmaker to drink. Lifting the roof off, one would have seen an interior just as perfectly detailed as the outside, with a potbellied stove and a casual litter of train-crew gear. The kit and its embellishments had cost fifteen dollars, but more than forty hours of exacting work had gone into making it look like a vector of industrial blight and a victim of managerial neglect.

Walter left the caboose on the main line while he backed the train into the siding – where a switch engine, property of the Mason Mining Company, had left three more hoppers full of coal. The mine, an even more ramshackle enterprise than the railroad that served it, had been christened to honor Katy's maiden name. He'd been hurt by her indifference to his whimsy. "If I really owned that mine, I'd sell it and build a respiratory clinic for the poor devils who work on your railroad," she'd said.

He sighed. He was uncomfortable with words, especially when he wanted to talk about deep things, with one so glib as Katy. The Mason Mining Co., with its pit-head structures and rickety offices built board by board with scale lumber, had been a way of telling her he loved her.

It would be so much easier to talk to her if she shared his hobby. She had seemed interested in it when they'd been in high school. She'd used to come down here almost every Saturday to help him build the models or run the trains. It had been easy to speak of deep, important things in an offhand way while they were both busy. Now she flitted off almost every night with the bright, brittle people he couldn't stand while he worked alone in the basement.

He should try once more to convince her that they ought to spend the month of August together at Painter Lake. They owned a lodge surrounded by a huge tract of woods, and they would be completely alone. It could be like a second honeymoon.

The lake had been named for an exploit of Walter's

great grandfather, Moses Burroughs. Hunting where the lodge now stood, he had shot the last mountain lion, or "painter," ever reported in the state. Walter's father, an avid hunter and gun collector, had considered that a great distinction. Walter never had. Maybe people in general hadn't thought it praiseworthy, either: they'd named the lake after the painter, not after Moses Burroughs.

He and Katy used to go there every summer, and she had sometimes been able to put aside her prudish ways in the isolation and swim nude. He could see her now, with the water beading like diamonds in the sun on her breasts. He wished he could recreate the happy innocence of those days, but he didn't know how to begin. Getting her alone and talking with her, that might be a start.

The telephone rang. Despite Katy's repeated suggestions, he had stubbornly refused to have an extension installed in the basement. Most callers would give up before he got halfway to the kitchen, and that was just fine with him. Katy knew his trick, though, and she would let it ring all night if necessary.

It kept ringing. He grudgingly put his engineer's cap aside and ran his hand through his thinning hair as he mounted the steps to the kitchen. As he climbed, he could hear the brisk patter of rain on the garbage cans outside the kitchen door. It must be Katy phoning, in need of a lift. He ran up the last steps.

He answered the phone as he always did when he thought he knew who was calling, with the word: "Yes?"

A man's voice, its tones rounded and overripened at some Ivy League school, proved him wrong: "Mr. Burroughs, if you please."

"Speaking."

"This is Quentin Swift." Walter already knew that, so he said nothing. "Dr. Swift, from the university. I believe we've spoken before."

Swift often called to remind Katy of cultural events, or to commend to her attention some exercise in unrelieved dreariness on the educational TV station. He was trying to get into her pants, of course, as any man would want to, but he was going about it in such a schoolmarmish way that Walter didn't consider him a threat.

"What do you want?" said Walter, who could be quite brusque on the telephone, but who always regretted it later.

"A few of us at the Library Society are going over to the Cobbles for drinks, and we wondered if Katy – if you and Mrs. Burroughs would join us."

"What does she say?"

"I beg your pardon?"

"I mean, does she want me to go over there, or to the library, or what? Isn't she there?"

If Swift had reacted a split second sooner, Walter wouldn't have guessed the truth, but he hesitated just a shade too long before answering: "She left before I had a chance to mention it to her."

Walter's lips felt strangely numb, and he had to force them to form words: "If she just left the library, she should be home before long. I'll give her your message."

"Yes. Thanks so much. Sorry to have disturbed you."

"Good night," Walter said and hung up.

He had felt comfortable in the certitude of routine: he was working on his railroad, Katy was playing intellectual with her friends. He was no longer comfortable. He was all alone in the vast house. He walked to the window. Gray veils of rain drifted past a distant streetlight. He thought of getting out his car and going to meet her on her way home. But he didn't know if she was on her way home. She hadn't been to the library at all. Swift had lied.

He felt most uncomfortable in the kitchen. Even though her culinary skills were limited to opening cans, she had made the room hers with characteristic touches. Plastic or metal surfaces had been disguised with paint in earth tones. The walls had been painted a burnt orange that had taken some getting used to. In his youth, the kitchen had been like a hospital room, flat white and stainless steel, and he had almost never entered it: it had been a den of coarse, cruel servants who spent their spare time plotting humiliations for him.

He didn't feel the impulse coming, but the next thing he knew he was kicking a chair across the room and shouting: "Fuck! Shit! God damn it! God *damn* it!"

He forced himself to be calm, but his hand still shook. He hadn't consciously analyzed the possibilities suggested by that phone call. He simply knew what was happening. Somewhere out in the rainy night, some man was fucking Katy. While he'd been playing with his toy trains, a stranger's hands had been sliding on his wife's naked skin. Someone else had been looking into the deer-soft darkness of her eyes, fondling the heaviness of her glossy hair. Were they naked on the bed of a motel, or were they half-clothed as they squirmed lustily in the confines of a car?

He could hear her voice: "Walter, I have to get up in the morning . . . . I have a headache, darling, really . . . . Please, I'm trying to sleep . . . . Not first thing in the morning, dear, *honestly. . . !* Not this afternoon, I want to grab a nap . . . It's my period, Walter, it just started . . ."

He was surprised to find that it actually hurt: it was a physical pain, even though he couldn't pinpoint the exact place. Maybe this proved the existence of the soul.

Maybe that was the part that hurt so much.

He went to their well-stocked bar. He seldom drank, and Katy only did when she was out with her witty friends. Some of the bottles had been stocked by his father. He took a bottle at random and half-filled an old-fashioned glass. He drained it and looked at the label on the bottle. It was scotch: Johnny Walker Black Label. He poured another. He took his drink to his study and dialed the number of the library. The phone rang twelve times, but no one answered. It was just as well, for he wouldn't have known what to say. He replaced the receiver on the hook.

She writhed beneath him, slim and strong and bare as an eel. "You're doing it, Walter, you're doing it . . . oh, oh, oh," she moaned in time to his thrusts.

Despite such theatrics, staged early in their marriage, he doubted that she'd ever known an orgasm. Sex seemed to repel her. Perhaps it was only that he repelled her. He went back to the bar and got the bottle, pouring a third drink as he returned to the study.

He listened attentively to the infrequent sounds of distant automobiles in the night. Someone would be bringing her home in a car. He would probably drop her off right at the front gate because of the rain. She would greet him with a story about the fascinating meeting that had lasted so long, about the lift some girl friend had given her. Perhaps, she wouldn't come into the house right away but would linger out in his car, risking a last kiss, letting him cop a last feel, breaking it up before she fell into the tingling fingers of reawakened lust. She would hurry up the long driveway with the sweat of someone else's hands still damp on her buttocks, with someone else's seed still fresh in her cunt.

He drank. Then he unlocked his desk and took out his revolver.

He owned a .38 caliber Smith & Wesson with a two-inch barrel, the type of gun popularly known as a belly-buster. He'd bought it secondhand long ago, and the white metal showed in spots where the bluing had worn away. It worked perfectly, though. He stared into the black hole of the muzzle and pulled the trigger. The hammer snapped on an empty chamber. He laughed. That was something you were never supposed to do with a gun. He did it again, knowing the gun was empty.

"But maybe it isn't, and maybe that's what you're hoping," he said aloud, pushing the pistol to the other side of the table as if the pistol itself were the thought that had tempted him.

He supposed he had taken out the pistol with the thought of staging a confrontation: I'll teach you to cheat on me. White faces contorted with horror behind a rainy windshield. O my God it's Walter. Bang. Bang.

No, just one "bang." He could never hurt Katy. But if he killed Katy's lover and bought his way out of the consequences, as he supposed he could do, he would still lose her. He couldn't kill himself. That would be lying dawn and letting them win, the sadistic servants and his malicious father, the boys who had beaten him, the pretty girls who had laughed at him, the workers who went "toot-toot" behind his back. Even with this pain and all his other troubles, there were a lot of things he wanted to do before he died.

He laughed. He had originally bought the gun with the idea that he needed it to protect Katy. He had known his own physical limitations, and he had feared the casual violence of the times. He often pictured her being raped by blacks or hippies who tied him up and made him watch. He was ashamed of those fantasies because they never failed to excite him.

She had gotten a good laugh out of it when he'd told

her why he'd bought the gun. She believed that a soft answer turneth away wrath, that a sincere desire to communicate could stop bullets. She didn't know that things walked abroad with the smiling faces of human beings, that twisted foulness could lurk in any human heart, perhaps because she had never looked deeply enough inside herself: For all her surface brightness, she wasn't a deep person, either in thought or feeling.

He had always considered her an exception to his rule, however. He had always believed her to be good and decent and modest. That was why he had so vehemently resisted Marjorie Corcoran's recent, vile suggestion. Even hinting at the idea to Katy would have been unthinkable. Now maybe it wouldn't. Katy was just a stinking whore, no better than Marjorie or Gretchen. She'd only had a better act, that was all.

Preoccupied, he'd forgotten to listen for cars. He heard footsteps. Before he could decide how to act or what to say, Katy stood in the door of his study.

"No movie?" she asked.

"I got involved in what I was doing downstairs."

She came forward into the light. He saw that she was soaked. Whenever he saw her like this, with her black hair plastered close to her head, he was always freshly dazzled by the beautiful bone structure of her face. She reminded him of the famous bust of Nefertiti; a sculpture he was familiar with only because she had once called his attention to the resemblance. Her wet dress clung to her body, and her erected nipples were visible. She hadn't worn a bra. More likely, she'd taken it off somewhere and forgotten it.

She started to say something, but then she laughed shortly, in uneasy surprise. He followed her eyes and saw the whisky bottle and the pistol on the table beside his easy chair. He realized that he looked like a character from one of those dismal Russian plays that

Quentin Swift encouraged her to watch on the educational channel.

"I was just checking it, you know, making sure it was empty," he said.

"The bottle?" she asked, holding it up to the light of his reading lamp. "Looks like you did a pretty good job. Can I have some?"

"Of course. Why didn't you call me for a lift?"

Leaving the room, she called back in a chillingly cheerful voice: "You know I love to walk in the rain."

That was true. She would go out of her way to do it, disdaining umbrellas and raincoats.

Not even thunder and lightning, which made him extremely uncomfortable, could stop her. He wished he had a nickel for every time she'd dragged him out and gotten him soaking wet before they were married. Since then, he'd managed to resist her invitations.

He wanted to believe that the sound of the rain outside had tempted her to leave the library early and that Swift, blinded by his own brilliance hadn't noticed her in the audience. Walter believed that a cleverer man than he was would have been able to determine the exact truth just by talking to her. He wished he could think up the kind of snappy, incisive questions that Dick Powell had asked in *Murder, My Sweet.*

"You want some ice cubes?" she asked, returning.

It was exasperating that she could say such prosaic things so easily. She should have stammered, averted her eyes from his accusing look. "Yeah, sure," he said. "Please."

As she poured herself a drink, he found the nerve to say: "Your boyfriend called."

Her hand didn't tremble, she didn't spill a drop; she just said: "Oh? Who might that be?"

"Quentin Swift."

She frowned. "I didn't see him tonight, not to speak

to," she said, brazenly meeting his eyes as she sat down in the chair opposite. "I sat in the back, and then I left early to walk in the rain. What did he want?"

There: the obvious explanation. But hearing his own theory drop so patly from her lips gave him no relief. She knew him too well; she knew exactly what he could be expected to believe. He couldn't have been more skeptical if she'd told him that she'd followed a white rabbit in a waistcoat down its hole.

"Why did he call?" she asked again.

"He wanted us to come to the Cobbles for a drink."

"If he was half as smart as he thought he was, he wouldn't be teaching in Armitage."

He wondered what had prompted that slur. She'd always spoken well of him before.

"Do you want to go?" he asked.

"It's late. And I thought you wanted to try some oral sex tonight."

"Huh?"

She picked up his pistol from the table and twirled it around her finger. With a look that could have been playful or sarcastic, he couldn't tell, she said: "You said before you wanted me to blow you. Wasn't that the word you used?"

"Cut it out, Katy," he said, and he paused to gulp the liquor remaining in his glass. "I said I was sorry about that, for being so crude, or whatever I was being. Stop teasing me. And quit playing with that gun, it's dangerous."

She stroked the muzzle against the fullness of her lower lip with allusive lubricity. "Come on, Walter, let me play with your gun," she giggled. "I'm not teasing you. I thought about what you said, and I want to try it. Have you changed your mind?"

He studied her suspiciously as he refilled his glass. He didn't dare rush headlong into what might prove to be a vicious trap. They'd always used to torment him like this in school, holding out some benefit that they would snatch away when he extended his hand. Katy had never teased him like that before. There were a lot of things Katy had never done before. She smiled at him, her head coyly cocked to one side, consciously trying to look seductive and succeeding impressively.

"I'll get out of my wet clothes while you sit there wrestling with your soul, Walter. I hope you make up your mind and come to bed before morning."

She stood up and let her colorful vest drop to the chair. She reached back to fumble with the fastenings of her shift. Her movements made her breasts thrust out, quivering beneath the near-transparency of the wet sill.

Shock, and the growing fear that she was making fun of him, immobilized him in his chair. Katy seldom made the first move in their sexual relations. When she did, it was usually when she was absolutely certain that he had other plans for the evening: He would patiently explain that he'd been waiting for months to see a particular movie, and she knew it, but she would fret and sulk and use his refusal as an excuse to resist his advances for the next couple of weeks. Maybe she was acting this way now only because she supposed he was too drunk to perform. If so, she was in for a surprise.

She pulled her dress over her head and tossed it in a wet wad on the rug. That was unlike her. She thought more of her hippie clothes; as he referred to them, than she did of any of her Dior originals. He wondered if she was drunk, or if she'd been smoking pot. Her friends from the Library Society all smoked it to enhance their fantasy of being bohemian intellectuals. But she didn't seem drunk or drugged. Apart from her unprecedented sexiness, she seemed perfectly normal.

"I want to take a bath first," she said, returning his eager gaze with a smile. "You come on up when you're finished thinking about it."

"I don't have to think about it," he said, getting out of his chair.

She slipped away when he reached for her. "You're the one who read the marriage manual, Walter, so you'll just have to tell me what to do," she said, mimicking a child's voice. "Anything you want."

He watched her walk from the room, so strangely unashamed of her nakedness. His eyes fixed on the delightfully undulant cheeks of her rosy buttocks. He could probably count the number of times he had seen her naked in a clear light, and he thought how lovely she was. It was a shame she had insisted from the first that they always make love with the lights out.

She turned at the door, a curious and unreadable expression in her dark eyes. He feasted on the rare sight of her bare breasts.

"Walter," she said, "do you know anybody named Corcoran?"

So much for his fantasies of being Dick Powell. Never in his life had a more frightening question been sprung on him so unexpectedly. Not even his father, a master of the art, had ever pulled one off that well. His drink fell to the floor. He averted his eyes.

"No, I don't think so," he said, making a show of retrieving the ice cubes from the rug. "Why?"

"A man named Corcoran stopped me on the street tonight. He works for you."

"That's where I heard the name before," he said, somewhat relieved to find she was talking about Sonny. "I got him hired as a favor to his – to his parole officer. You shouldn't talk to people like that, for God's sake. He's crazy as a bedbug."

"Maybe," she said. "He thinks you're a genius."

On that line, she left.

It occurred to him that they hadn't exchanged a single kiss since her return. It seemed an odd preparation for lovemaking, especially from her: just taking off her clothes and announcing what she planned to do.

"I love you," he called after her, but she had apparently gone out of earshot, for he heard no response.

He poured another drink and listened to the rain. The sound was crisper now, more insistent. The sound was soon obscured by the clanking and muffled roar of the ancient plumbing as she began to fill the tub in her upstairs bathroom.

Another man had been fucking her, and that's why she thought she needed a bath. He squelched the thought instantly, angry with himself for doubting her. Swift hadn't seen her because she'd sat at the rear of the gathering, and she'd left early to take a walk in the in the rain. She wouldn't act as she had if she'd just been with a lover.

He got up and put his pistol away. Who was her lover? Sonny Corcoran? He laughed. He topped off his drink and carried the bottle back to the bar. It was Swift, of course, who thought he knew everything, who patronized him and sneered at him. The phone call had been the kind of sadistic joke they had always played on him. Swift had called to make sure he was aware of Katy's infidelity, to rub his nose in it, but to misdirect his suspicions. He wasn't as smart as he thought, as Katy herself had said. She was probably mad at him because he'd come too soon. That was the only reason she wanted him, her husband: to take up where her lover had left off. Or maybe she was merely curious to see how many men she could accommodate in one evening.

He wrenched his mind away from those filthy

thoughts. Katy wasn't like that. She wasn't Marjorie, for Christ's sake! A person like Marjorie was a contagious loathsomeness. Contact with her had corrupted him. He had been able to see the evil in the world before, but now the whole world was evil, even Katy, because he saw the world as Marjorie did.

He remembered his trains. He walked cautiously down the basement stairs, acknowledging that he had drunk too much. Not enough to make him unable to accept Katy's offer, though. She was going to do something for him that she had never done before.

"Se never did it to anyone before," he said aloud, answering a phantom accusation that whispered in the rain against the basement windows.

The engine awaited him, humming, backed into the siding of the Mason Mining Co. The caboose sat on the main line where the imaginary brakemen had left it. It was all so neat, so logical, so unlike the world he was forced to live in. Even the decay and the filth were only illusions.

He switched off the power. Something tickled his cheek. He brushed at it with his finger, and he was surprised to discover that it was a tear. The questions and doubts and fears that he had been suppressing so successfully abruptly boiled over in a strangled cry: "Where was she tonight?"

Before he recognized what he was doing, before he could reverse the irrevocable act, his fist came down like God's – and flattened the caboose into a pile of splinters.

Chapter Seven

Even by the liberal standards of the circle of friends that she shared with Katy Burroughs, Suzy Decker was considered a dissolute woman. Intriguingly so, of course. Women who might deplore her antics in private sought her company so that they might get the latest gossip about her straight from the source; being seen with her gave them a sensation of adventurousness and sophistication, as if by osmosis.

Walter hated her, which made him unique among the men Katy knew. At one of the rare cocktail parties to which she had managed to drag him, Suzy Decker had tried to add him to her entourage of male admirers. Barely had she begun to bat her eyelashes when Walter turned his back on her and walked away. On the way home, Katy had been subjected to a grumbling account of the "cheap little flirt" who had kept popping up wherever he turned.

So, having told him that she planned to have lunch and do some shopping with Suzy, she felt confident that he wouldn't question Suzy about it later, in case he was suspicious: That was nonsense, of course: you had to have intelligence and imagination to be suspicious, and Walter had neither. But you couldn't be too careful, either.

He had scared her out of her wits the other night. Seeing the gun and the bottle, she was instantly certain that he knew the truth and that he planned to stage some melodramatic scene from one of his old movies. She was even more certain when he told her that that idiot Quentin had tipped him off. But she'd been entirely wrong. It was pure coincidence that he'd picked that night to get drunk and play with his stupid gun, as he sometimes did, pretending that he was Humphrey Bogart.

But that false alarm had served to make her doubly cautious. She was having lunch with Suzy, but she didn't plan a shopping trip with her.

"Everybody's talking about you," Suzy said, exploring her crabmeat salad suspiciously before tasting it. "It's getting to the point where I'm feeling neglected."

Katy went numb, but she managed to laugh. "Oh? And what are they saying?"

"That there's a man in your life," she whispered portentously. "Who is he?"

"Walter, of course. Don't be silly."

"Toot-toot," Suzy said contemptuously, as she always did when Walter's name came up ever since he'd spurned her advances at the cocktail party. "Don't try to give me that shit. I know. Why did you ask me to lunch if not to tell me some deep, dark secret that you want me to spread all over town?"

Katy couldn't help smiling. Subconsciously, that might have been her reason. She was itching to confide in someone, although Suzy would have been the worst possible choice. Maybe not. Despite what she'd just said, and despite the fact that she told often shockingly detailed stories about her own adventures, Suzy had never told her anyone else's secrets. But no. She could tell no one.

"I hate to disappoint you, Suzy, but there's nothing to tell. I can't imagine what you might have heard. Maybe somebody mistook you for me."

Suzy laughed at Katy's allusion. They were both slim brunettes who wore their hair long and straight; they were both fond of bright colors, ankle-length skirts, peasant blouses. One night at the crowded opening of a local artist's show, a slightly nearsighted woman had rushed up to Suzy with an effusive greeting meant for Katy, discovering only at the last moment that she was about to embrace the woman who was diving with her wayward husband.

"Not this time, kiddo," Suzy said. "I wasn't the one who told my husband I was going to hear Quentin Swift babble about the Ring of the Niebelungs. And I wasn't the one who didn't show up."

"It was *The Lord of the Rings,*" Katy corrected. "And who said I didn't show up?"

"*You* know who said you didn't show up. He said you'd been leading him on. He planned to transform you into a palpitating, mindless puddle of lust with his brilliant insights about Frodo the Hobbit. And you didn't even show. He was so pissed off he called and told your husband."

"You mean he did that on purpose? And then he told you about it? What a son-of-a-bitch!"

"Shh! I refuse to be seen in your company if you're going to scream naughty words in restaurants."

Katy shrank and concentrated on her chef's salad with total absorption. She hadn't realized that she'd spoken so loudly. People were actually staring.

"And," Suzy continued, "I'll thank you not to talk that way about the man I currently love."

"Oh?" Katy said, unable to hide a touch of vexation.

"Well, someone had to console the poor lamb, and

you couldn't expect his wife to do it, could you?"

Katy said seriously: "I think that was why I didn't – I mean, a married man –"

"It's the only kind," Suzy interrupted. "They always have someplace to go when you don't want them underfoot. But all that is beside the point. Who is he?"

Katy carefully refilled her glass of Perrier, stalling. She ought to feel relieved. Nobody had witnessed the events in the park, as she'd originally feared. She might give out a story that contained part of the truth, since it was a part Walter already knew something about.

"I wasn't with anyone, really, in that sense. I mean, I hadn't planned anything."

"That's the best way to do it," Suzy said smugly.

"Stop it, Suzy! I'm going to tell you the truth, and there's nothing at all to it. On the way to the library that night, a kind of eccentric, I guess you'd call him, came up to me with a wild story about how much he admired Walter, what a genius he thought he was."

"Oh, Jesus. Have mercy." She laughed so long and hard that it was her turn to be stared at. At last she managed to choke: "Not Sonny Corcoran?"

Katy was astonished. "You know him?"

"He lives down the street from me. One day last year, just after I moved in, he pounded on my door and told me my lawn needed mowing. I said I was pining away for some big, strong young man to come and do it, and he volunteered. He wouldn't even take money for it, but I lured him in for some lemonade, and one thing led to another, like in those books about aristocratic ladies and their gardeners. It looks like we're even, dear. I stole your boyfriend while you were busy stealing one of mine."

"It wasn't like that at all, Suzy. We talked. He wanted to tell me how much he admired Walter. Does he go around telling that to everyone, I wonder?"

"I don't know. He used to tell me. I'd always say 'toot-toot,' but I don't think he ever figured out why. I got the feeling that it wouldn't be a good idea to contradict his opinion directly." Suzy looked as if she were about to add something else but thought better of it.

Katy knew what it was. She asked: "Did he ever tell you that Walter – that he thought Walter was his father?"

"Now that you mention it," Suzy said, smiling wryly, "yes."

"But it's not possible, is it? He must be at least twenty-three or –"

"He fooled me, too," Suzy cut in. "It made me feel like a dirty old lady when I found out that I'd been fucking somebody who would have been in high school, if they hadn't expelled him. He's only eighteen now."

"Good heavens," Katy said. She didn't know which shocked her more: her own mistake about Raymond's age, or the possibility that Walter might indeed be the boy's father. "But Walter and I – we were going steady then. He was scared to death of girls. He wouldn't've . . ."

Suzy took up the slack when Katy's voice trailed off "It's the shy ones who fool you. And Ma Corcoran always shared our own passion for young stuff." She ignored Katy's angry glare and continued: "But I'm sure he's not going around telling everyone that Walter is his father, if that worries you. With me, it was one of those late-night confidences that you don't want to hear. And he told you, I guess, because you're – his what? His stepmother?"

She didn't join in Suzy's laughter. "What worries me – it doesn't worry me, really, it's just that I can't imagine Walter, the way he was then –"

"The Little Engine That Could," Suzy managed to gasp, and this time they both screamed with laughter.

The waiter's manner was markedly distant when he took their order for dessert and coffee, and Katy sat up straight and made a firm resolution to behave in a more dignified way. It was lucky they'd both decided on Perrier water instead of their customary carafe of white wine.

"This Mrs. Corcoran – Raymond told me a horror story about her making him have sex while she watched."

"Yeah, with his sisters. I –" Suzy stopped, observing Katy's shock. "No, I guess he didn't tell you that one. Whatever he told you is probably true. Ma is the town's most colorful character. Nothing inhuman is alien to her."

"She must be a *monster!* How could Walter – ?"

"Oh, she was quite a dish when she was in her twenties. I remember her going around with some of the high school hotshots. She used to wear frilly dresses and – big picture hats. Now she stomps around like a bull dyke in Army surplus pants and lumberjack shirts. Do you suppose we could write her up for *Reader's Digest?*"

"Well, there you are," Katy said. "You said you saw her with the high school hotshots. Not with Walter –"

"The only reason I saw *her* was because I was noticing *them.* From what I heard, she wasn't at all selective. The silly part of the story is trying to pin Sonny's paternity on Walter when she must have screwed half the senior class: the male half."

"Sonny – I mean, Raymond – must have some reason for believing it."

"Not necessarily. Your new boyfriend isn't wrapped too tight, as you may have noticed. And Walter is the ideal father-figure for any moron to identify with, toot-toot."

Katy believed that they would be able at least to make a dignified exit from the restaurant. But as they were weaving their way through the tables, Suzy, behind her, began to quote: "I think I can, I think I can, I know I can, I know I can." Gasping and sputtering, they had to hold each other for support as they staggered through the door.

Having said good-bye to Suzy, Katy went to her car: a Mercedes-Benz she'd bought last year because she'd liked the look of it in a showroom window. She hadn't even considered the price, and it came as a mild shock when the salesman calculated it. If she ever decided to leave Walter, she would be giving up the magical power of pointing to anything that caught her eye and having it.

Odd, Walter's money had never meant a thing to her, or so she'd always believed. She was sure it hadn't meant anything when they'd lived together in a trailer, impoverished by his father's whim. But now she was used to wealth. The need for it had grown in her unnoticed, recognized for the first time only now, when she was thinking of giving it up. She wouldn't starve, of course. With her property settlement and alimony, she would probably be quite well off. But the real money and its source – the mill – would be beyond her grasp. All those high-priced lawyers and accountants that Walter had always paid to do his thinking for him had coldbloodedly foreseen the possibility of a divorce and protected the Young Master against it.

How much did a cop make in a town like this? A couple of hundred dollars a week, probably, and all the apples he could steal. She should have fallen for a tricky accountant who could have drawn up papers that would strip Walter to the bone when she duped him into signing them. All a cop had was his badge.

And, of course, his gun.

She laughed at her own crazy imagination. One of Walter's all-time favorites was *Double Indemnity,* a film in which an insurance agent conspires with a woman to murder her husband for the death benefits.

Walter had a lot of insurance.

Her timing couldn't have been better, she reflected. Just as she was entertaining these naughty thoughts, she arrived at the address on Water Street that Frank had given her. It was a garage. He lived upstairs, and his battered red convertible lived downstairs. According to one person to whom she had – with studied casualness – dropped his name, Frank was kept in a state of suspended animation in a box beneath police headquarters, to be activated by the command: "Dill!"

She could call the police about a prowler some night when Walter was out, Frank would answer the call and –

Stop it! she told herself firmly. She didn't hate Walter; not in any real sense of the word, and that was the only circumstance in which she could imagine herself killing someone. She certainly couldn't do it for money. She was simply sick and tired of Walter, that was all; that didn't even prevent her from being fond of him in a way.

It was odd. After Frank had demolished her misconception of what sex was all about, sex with Walter had improved dramatically. That had nothing to do with Walter, who was still his same, dull self, in bed or out of it. It had partly to do with her own lack of feeling for him. No longer particularly caring about him, she was able to shed all her previous inhibitions and let herself go completely. Walter was totally bemused. He seemed to want her all the time now, and she would submit to his advances and follow his suggestions with amused detachment. They'd done it in the shower last night, an unheard-of debauch.

When Frank opened the door to her knock and she saw him again, all thoughts of Walter were swept out of her mind. She felt like one of those see-through plastic models of a human being, with all the veins and muscles and nerve delineated in different colors; but all of her veins and muscles and nerves were delineated in various subtle intensities of need and want.

Later, while Frank smoked a cigarette and smiled smugly at his water-stained ceiling, she sat up on the daybed and examined the room for the first time. It was as impersonal as a motel room, and far sleazier. The walls were painted a dull, institutional green. The pictures on the walls, still-lifes of fruit and flowers, must have come with the place. It seemed to be furnished chiefly with someone's old lawn furniture: wrought-iron tables painted white, a couple of chairs with weather-beaten redwood frames, and plastic cushions in mismatching floral patterns. The floor was covered with linoleum, worn down to its black backing in trails that led to the comically antique stove and the bathroom cubicle. It wasn't all that different from a box beneath the police station.

"I didn't know the Salvation Army had a fire sale," she said.

"Coming down from the big house to make fun of the poor folks, eh? You ought to be ashamed of yourself, you bloodsucking capitalist oppressor."

She wasn't sure how he'd take it, but she wanted to say it: "I could fix it up for you, with some furniture and –"

"That's kind of you," he said, with a smile that relieved much of her embarrassment. "But there's no point. I don't plan to stay here any longer than I have to."

Prowling around the room, she found some personal

touches: a few books carelessly stored in paper boxes, mostly history and science; a stereo and some records. The records, she was surprised to find, were Mozart chamber works. She knew that her surprise stemmed from snobbery, and she resolved to keep a more open mind. Of course there were his clothes, too: a pipe-rack full of spiffy sports coats and suits, all cleaned and neatly pressed. Maybe his dry-cleaning bill kept him broke.

"But why do you have to?" she asked.

"Alimony. Child support."

"What happened?"

"Read about it in Joseph Wambaugh," he said, then added hastily: "No, I'm sorry, that was a flippant answer."

"You couldn't prove it by me. I never heard of him."

"He was a policeman who became a writer. One of his favorite subjects is the high divorce rate among policemen. A cop's hours make it hard to keep a marriage going." He smoked silently for awhile, still looking at the ceiling, while she curled into one of his lawn chairs and regretted it: the plastic felt clammy against her skin.

"They have a high suicide rate, too," he said, "but that's because they all own guns. Psychiatrists do, too, and they have access to pills. And we both have to sweep up the shit, one way or another; maybe that's the common denominator."

She wondered if he was being profound or just reciting something he'd read. It had taken her a long time to learn that Walter's best lines came from old movies.

"Is it hard to kill someone?"

"No. We all go down pretty easy."

"I meant, is it hard for you? Emotionally. Whatever."

"I know what you meant, and I was being flippant

again. Women often ask it, and I don't like it."

"I'm not 'women.' Or am I?"

"The answer to both questions is, No. It's not hard when I have to do it."

"I know from experience that the second part of that answer doesn't refer to me."

"You have a dirty mind," he said, laughing, and she warmed to him: Walter could never have followed her in such verbal play.

"Do you enjoy killing people?" she asked.

He rolled his legs off the daybed to sit up and look at her. The sunlight falling on his body emphasized something not easily noticed, that he was incredibly hairy. If the fur on his legs and body hadn't been so light, she might have compared him to a gorilla. Walter was as smooth as an egg.

"No," he said coldly, "I don't."

"Don't be angry with me. I'm trying to know you, don't you understand? And you're not like any of the men I've met."

"Because I've killed people? Maybe I should wear some kind of mark on my forehead, huh?"

She sighed. "You're also the touchiest man I ever met, on this subject."

"Like I said, it's because I've heard these questions before."

"And you seem to suggest that I'm asking them out of idle curiosity, or to give myself a wicked little shiver. I'm not. As I said, I want to know you." His eyes softened slightly, so she went on: "The reason I asked, really – it looked to me like you were enjoying yourself when you were beating up Raymond Corcoran."

"Fair enough, rich lady. Now I've got one: you seemed to enjoy watching it. I might even go so far as to say that it turned you on."

She looked away. "Ouch," she said. "Okay. I'm asking you for honest answers, so I guess I have to try to give you one. That's partly right. I found out something about myself that I didn't know. I didn't like it, either. I don't plan to look for kicks that way. It's something I have to overcome."

"That sounds pretty honest," he said. "I'm afraid it's built into us, men and women, the way we are. Overcoming it is what laws and constitutions and Mozart and all the good parts of civilization are all about. It's what my job can be, at its best, and that's why I've stuck with it."

"Do we salute the flag now, or are you going to tell me why you enjoyed beating the shit out of Raymond?"

He laughed loudly. "I wasn't trying to bullshit you, honest. Not completely. I do believe something like that, although I never tried to think it all the way through." He stood up and walked to the window, looking out as he spoke. "As for Raymond, he's a scumbag, his mother is a scumbag, his sisters were scumbags. If he had a dog and a cat, they'd be scumbags, too. Keeping their kind of filth in line, that's my job. But it's no reason to beat him up – no, I take that back, it's no reason to enjoy doing it." He brooded for a moment, then turned to look at her. "I think Raymond is the guy the papers call the Full Moon Maniac."

"When you said that, that night, I thought you were just trying to scare me."

"I've got nothing. Just opportunity – he was up in the hills on those nights, I know it – but I can't even prove that. He's got a history of violence. I found out he's even got some sex crimes on his juvenile sheet – chickenshit stuff, but everybody's got so start somewhere."

"Considering his mother, it's probably to his

credit –"

"I'd be even more willing to believe that it's his mother, armed with a dildo. Raymond is mean, but he's not as vicious as Ma."

"What's a dildo?"

He looked at her oddly. "It's an artificial dick. But Ma –"

"Wait a minute," she interrupted. "Raymond is her dildo. He told me the other night that his mother forces him – well, no, *encourages* him to make love to somebody named Gretchen while she watches. And just today – Christ, it makes me sick to say it! – somebody else told me that she used to make him do the same thing with his own sisters." He sat down on the bed and looked thoughtful for a moment. "Who told you that?" he said at last.

"It was in confidence –"

"Don't give me that! We're talking about rape, and murder, and the fact that I'm betting everything I've got on Sonny Corcoran. Who was it?"

He didn't seem to realize that he'd just revealed a lot about himself that his set speeches hadn't. He stared hard at her.

"A woman named Suzy Decker."

"And how does she know?"

"Raymond told her. They were lovers."

He smiled unpleasantly. "Is that what it's called?"

"Sometimes," she said, getting up to join him on the bed.

As he began to caress her, she asked: "Would you kill my husband?"

"Why?"

"So we can live together with his money."

"No."

"That's what I thought you'd say," she laughed, happily, And she relaxed into the circle of his strong arms.

Chapter Eight

Frank found Steve LaRue working on the engine of a van painted with streaming fireballs in front of his parents' house on Division Street.

"Oh," he said sourly, when he looked up to see Frank; then he added a grudging, "Hi."

"Yours?" Frank asked, standing back as if to admire the fiery mural.

"Yeah, I just got it. Nice, huh?"

"Beautiful. Now they won't be able to lock you in the trunk."

Steve laughed easily. "That's the real beauty of it." He walked briskly to the back and flung open the doors. "See? We can lock ourselves in. Just go someplace and park, and nobody can bother you."

The rear of the van was cushioned like a padded cell with deep, shaggy carpet. It was appointed with colorful pillows, an imitation fur rug, and stereo speakers. The ceiling was a mirror, and there was a mirror on either wall.

"Staying home in bed is even safer," Frank said.

"Yeah, tell that to my folks. I'm twenty years old, man, but they'd shit a brick if I brought a girl home to spend the night. My old man still yells at me if I stay out late. My mother thinks this van is like something out of the last days of the Roman Empire, and the whole world is going to go to hell because I bought it."

"Then I'll know who to blame when it does." While Steve was still laughing politely, Frank asked: "You hear much from Betty these days?"

Steve shrugged and gave him a surly look. Then he said, almost shouting: "What the hell is this, we going to keep holding class reunions? I answered your questions three times, I answered questions for five other guys, and last week some captain came around with the same damned questions."

"Calm down. I just wanted to ask you if you've remembered anything more about the woman."

"No, I – shit, what woman? What are you talking about?"

"See, that's how it works. We question you twenty times, and on the twenty-first time, you screw up. Why didn't you tell me about the woman in the first place?"

"Look, man, Betty got raped, I got roughed up, we both got thrown into a trunk where we nearly froze to death. Those are crimes, aren't they? What difference does the other shit make?"

Even though he didn't feel reasonable at this moment, Frank tried to sound so: "The difference it makes is, that all this time we've been looking for one guy. Now you tell us he had a woman with him. We had the scene of the goddamned crime staked out for months, we had patrols and spot checks, they were all looking for one man, and maybe this fucking *couple* was breezing past them all the time, just because you decided a piece of information was unimportant."

"Let go," Steve croaked, and only then did Frank realized that he was no longer sounding reasonable and was holding the young man a few inches off the ground by his throat.

"Okay, tell me. And tell it right this time," Frank said, dropping him.

"Shit," Steve said, rubbing his neck. He reached for a cigarette and lit it with shaking hands before he began: "You know the first part, Betty and I were in the front seat of my car on an old road near Sutton's Pond. We were both dressed, we were mostly just talking. Then up pops this guy at the window in a wool hat with eye-holes. He has a gun, a revolver, just like your .38 that you showed me. He tells us to get out of the car. Then he locks me in the trunk."

Steve took another long drag of his cigarette and said, "Here's where it gets different from what I told you. I was in the trunk maybe ten minutes when it opens up again. The guy tells me to get out, and I see he has somebody with him."

"The woman."

"I didn't know it then. She was tall, about my height, but not nearly as tall as the man. They were both wearing down jackets. She had a hat over her face, too, only it was a regular ski mask, with a design on it. She could have been a man or a woman or a grizzly bear in that outfit. Anyway, I thought, 'Holy fuck, they killed Betty, and now it's my turn.' So when the man told me to take off my clothes, I did it. Then he tied up my hands with clothesline and shoved me into the back seat of the car. He went away, and the other one got in with me. It freaked me out when she pulled down her pants, because I still thought she was a man, some kind of pervert. Then I saw it was a woman. She opened up her jacket next, and she didn't have anything under it. She had big tits, real nice ones, but they didn't do a thing for me under the circumstances. I was cold, and I was scared shitless."

"What did she say?"

"Nothing. Up until then, she hadn't said a word. I kept talking, though, I couldn't stop, asking her what she wanted and what was going to happen and I don't know what else. Then she grabbed my prick and started playing with it. Nothing happened, it just stayed absolutely limp. She had a nice body, but I don't think I could've got it up for Raquel Welch at that point. So she says, 'Shut up and relax.'"

"Could you recognize her voice again?"

"Shit, no. She spoke in a loud whisper, a hiss. It was the creepiest thing I ever heard, I still get nightmares about it, but it was a voice that anybody could have made.

"So anyway, I said, 'Come on, this isn't going to work.' And she said –" here he imitated the reptilian hiss – "'Maybe this will,' and she went down on me."

"In her ski mask?"

"She rolled it up from her chin, but she did it when she lowered her head. I didn't see any part of her face. She did it for a while, but that didn't work; either. So she got up and 'Okay, stud, you can eat me, if that's all you're good for.'"

"Still whispering?"

"Yeah. I didn't feel like eating her, either, so she grabbed me by the neck and pulled me down. She had strong legs, I mean, real strong. She got a lock on my head and kept me down there for an hour. My mouth was sore for a week after."

"She say anything?"

"Yeah, instructions, like 'Faster!' or 'Lick it up higher!' but still in that whisper. She made a lot of noise whenever I got to her, but it was like grunts and groans. Sometimes it sounded like I was being held prisoner in a veterinary hospital. But I couldn't recognize her from that."

"What happened then?"

"She had enough. I had more than enough. Christ! I used to like to eat pussy, but to this day, the thought of doing it turns my stomach. Anyway, she pulled me out of the car and opened the trunk. I thought I was home free, but at the last minute she pulls out this pig-sticker, like the biggest bowie knife I ever saw, and holds the blade against my balls. 'If you can't use it,' she says, 'maybe you don't need it.' I don't know what I said; but I know I did a lot of talking. Finally she put the knife away without saying anything and shoved me into the trunk. I was too scared even to ask her to let me put my clothes on, even though I was freezing my ass off by this time.

"Maybe a half-hour went by, I don't know, and then the man came back with Betty. He put her in the trunk and laid all that shit on us I told you about, calling her dirty names and telling me what I ought to do with her while we were waiting for help."

"Had she seen the woman?"

"I'm pretty sure she didn't. She talked a lot, she told me the stuff he did to her, but she didn't mention the woman."

"And why didn't you tell anyone about the woman?"

"Why do you suppose? It was embarrassing, for Christ's sake! How would you feel, getting raped by a woman? I didn't want all that stuff in the paper, about how I couldn't get it up, or how she made me go down on her for an hour. Christ, you would have had a great time telling jokes about it at the cop shop."

Frank studied him sourly, but Steve was right: he was tempted to laugh even now. His complaints were ironically the same as those of every female rape victim he'd ever interrogated.

"Give me a description," Frank said.

"Of what?" Steve laughed. "Okay, a great body,

maybe five – ten or eleven. She was built solid, so maybe she weighed as much as one-fifty. I'd guess her measurements at thirty-eight, twenty-eight, forty."

Frank hesitated to write that down. "You're pretty goddamned observant."

"I'm not making this up," Steve said, injured. "Like I said, she had a great body, and I notice them when I see them. I still kick myself when I think how I wasn't able to do anything about it."

Frank wrote down the measurements. "Any scars, moles?"

"No."

"An appendix scar?"

"No."

"You sure?"

"Absolutely."

"You're amazing. What color was her hair?"

"Man, I didn't see . . ." Steve hesitated, then snickered. "Oh. Yeah. Dark, that's all I can say. I couldn't say if it was brown or black. Dark brown is what I would guess."

"You saw her eyes, too."

"They were light, I think. Blue, gray, I couldn't say for sure. It was nighttime, and she had this mask on, and I wasn't looking at her eyes."

"You saw her hands and feet," Frank said, trying not to put any extra stress on the statement.

"She kept her boots on. Hiking boots. And hands are hands."

No they aren't, you jerk, he wanted to say, but he kept silent as his first real witness fell down at the key point. Steve LaRue only noticed those things about a woman that he wanted to notice. He couldn't hang Ma on this description anyway, with or without the hands. It would have been interesting to arrange a line-up for Steve, though; they would have made legal history.

Closing his notebook and putting it away, Frank asked, "You know the Corcorans?"

"In the next block. Sure."

"What's the smile for?"

Steve shrugged, and the smile seemed to broaden against his will. "Nothing."

"If you know a funny story about them, tell me. I could use a good laugh. Up until now, the funniest thing I could think of was taking you down to headquarters and booking you for suppressing evidence and giving false information to a police officer."

"You wouldn't do that! Would you?"

"Tell me the story, and maybe I'll forget about it."

"I told you, it's nothing. It's just that Ma Corcoran gave me my first piece of ass, that's all. So I smile when you mention her, that's all."

"You were in bed with Ma Corcoran."

"Yeah, that's what I just told you. Maybe ten or a dozen times."

"And hasn't it ever occurred to you, when you're having wet dreams about your glamorous rapist, that she fits Ma's description?"

Steve laughed loudly. His laughter tapered off when Frank didn't join him.

"Look, the last time I screwed Ma was six years ago: And this woman was younger than Ma was then."

"How can you tell? You didn't see her face, you didn't even notice her hands, and those are about the only sure ways you chin tell. Did she show you her birth certificate?"

"I can tell, man! This chick's skin was real tight and smooth. Her tits stuck right up and said hello. Ma was OFD six years ago, but now she looks like Raggedy Ann in drag. She's let herself go to pieces."

"I saw her in her skin the other night, and she looked just fine to me. The only improvement I could think of would be a ski mask."

"Well, you're older than I am, man, and maybe you're not as particular," Steve said earnestly, not meaning his words to be offensive. "Dumpy, that's the word for Ma."

"If you hit on her, you'd get a big surprise, believe me."

"Yeah, she'd stomp me. We didn't part the best of friends," Steve said glumly, but Frank could see that he'd kindled a spark of interest.

Frank was undecided how far he should push this. Even if Steve could identify Ma from what he'd seen, no prosecutor in his right mind would try to bring such evidence into court. For that matter, any identification that Steve might make would probably be worthless as evidence, now that Frank had suggested Ma's name to him. But Frank believed that he'd gotten closer to the truth; and once the truth was known, the evidence could be arranged to fit it.

When Steve spoke next, Frank saw that he didn't have to push his idea any further. He had succeeded in stirring up Steve's curiosity. "Like I said, Ma is no longer my biggest fan. And Sonny hates my guts. He's all the time telling me not to work on my cars out in the street; it destroys the tone of the neighborhood. Whenever I see him coming, I pick up a wrench. Maybe you could loan me one of your guns for when I visit Ma, huh?"

"Just be nice to him. Tell him you'll help water his flowers. Or go when he's not home."

"Who said I was going?" Steve said, looking shocked that the project had developed this far.

"Well, you do what you think is right. Let me tell you something, though. Even if you were a little late coming up with it, this is the best lead we've had yet. I'd see that you got a lot of the credit if it helps. Every girl in town would recognize you from your picture in the paper, the guy who caught the Full Moon Maniac."

"Yeah," Steve said thoughtfully. "As it is now, all the girls in town recognize me, but most of them run the other way."

"Whatever you do, keep in touch," Frank said, turning back to his car. "Anything more you might remember –"

"I know. But you got everything now. Maybe you should tell the captain, so he doesn't come around tomorrow with the same questions."

"Yeah," Frank called. "I'll do that."

The captain had been keeping Frank busy, and Frank had been trying to look that way. In addition to the knifing at the French Club, he was supposed to be investigating a hit-and-run accident, the burglary of a doctor's office on High Street, and a series of armed holdups at late-closing grocery stores and filling stations. His mornings were not his own, though, since LaPlante had assigned him to stake out an all-night gas station that hadn't yet been hit.

Actually, the French Club knifing had been solved, but Frank was keeping the solution to himself. Angelique had stayed at the bar after he'd left, and he'd persuaded her to tell him the name of the knifer. The next time the captain got on his back, he would make that arrest to keep LaPlante quiet for a while.

The stakeout was the most frustrating assignment. Screwball identifications notwithstanding, the only way he would ever get Ma and Sonny would be to catch them in the act; and he could only do that by tailing them. Instead, he was now spending his evenings crouched under the counter of a filling station.

He had done the next best thing – no, it wasn't the next best thing at all, it was the worst possible alternative, but it was the only one he had – by enlisting

Ronnie Elkins to watch the Corcoran house. Ronnie was the only cop dumb enough to believe, as Frank had told him, that such off-duty work without pay would help him get promoted to the detective division. He was also the only cop who didn't seem to know that Frank bad been pulled off the Maniac investigation. Frank had told Bonnie that the surveillance of the Corcorans was top secret, and he was sure that Ronnie wouldn't endanger his new image as an undercover agent by talking about it.

It wouldn't last, though. Ronnie was working the noon-to-eight shift this week, ideal for Frank's purposes. If Frank coached him well enough, he might pull it again next week by pleading some urgent personal business; but maybe not. And the full moon was due again next week.

Frank had gambled so much on Sonny now that he was almost willing to consider abandoning the stakeout next week to stick with him. He could have talked his way out of his earlier suppression of the evidence that Ma had been at Sutton's Pond on the night of the last crime by pinning the blame on Ronnie's confusion, perhaps. But if it came out that he was suppressing the conversation he'd just had with Steve LaRue, he would be kicked off the force. He could even be hit with a criminal charge, if LaPlante was in the mood to push it. Then there was his misuse of Ronnie, which probably violated some Mickey Mouse departmental rule. And his handling of that knifing, he might as well add that to the total he had riding on Sonny.

And on Ma, thanks to Katy. Even on the day of that fateful conversation, he'd still had a few lingering doubts about Sonny; but her line about Sonny being Ma's dildo had washed them away. Sonny wasn't bright enough or vicious enough to be the Maniac, but Ma was.

Perverts, Frank had found, were like drug addicts: they needed ever-increasing doses of their favorite poison. Masochists who started out by asking for a friendly little spanking often ended by killing themselves in gruesomely inventive ways. Ma's special kick was voyeurism. No longer satisfied with watching Sonny screw his sisters or Gretchen Slovak, she'd imagined a new source of fun: watching him rape somebody. From there maybe it had been a short step to getting a thrill out of watching him kill somebody.

Frank was inclined to believe that Ma had taken a more active role in that part of it, though. Maybe she could never have the only thing in life she really wanted, a dick; but she could pull a trigger as well as the next man. She could start a fire, too. Frank could see it so clearly in his imagination that he knew it was the way it must have happened: Ma scolding Sonny for his poor marksmanship; then, while the wounded kids were screaming in the trunk of the Pontiac, stepping forward to flick her Bic.

Any psychiatrist would believe he'd died and gone to heaven when they dragged a straitjacketed Ma Corcoran, foaming at the mouth, into his office. That was one of the reasons why he, and not LaPlante; had to stop Sonny and Ma. He had to make certain that she wouldn't be stalking the streets again in five or ten years, after paying her debt to Sigmund Freud.

Of course, there was a bright side to all this. Assuming he failed to stop the Corcorans, assuming he got kicked off the force and charged with obstructing justice, he could always murder Katy's husband and live happily ever after as the kept man of the richest woman in Armitage. He laughed so hard at this absurdity that he was forced to slow his car to keep it under control.

At thirty-eight, Frank had been firmly convinced

that falling in love was something that only stupid kids did. Anyone beyond his early twenties who professed to fall in love was practicing an exercise in self-deception. Those curious reactions he remembered from adolescence – the pleasant vertigo, the ache of need inside, the trembling of the knees at the sight of his beloved – they were as dead and gone and incapable of resurrection as the bones of a dinosaur. To sit alone and repeat a name, to get a thrill from writing it down on a piece of paper, to feel a tingle when it was mentioned in his presence: those practices had been misplaced along the line with his football trophies and his picture from the senior prom.

Well, he'd been wrong. Katy Burroughs – he loathed that name, he always thought of her secretly as Katy Mason, never attached to that wretched man – had proven him wrong.

Like all people in love, they had a game, something that only they shared, something that could fill any moment with laughter. Their game was called Let's Snuff Walter.

He had been reluctant to play at first. He had suspected that she'd been only half-kidding. She had finally convinced him that it was a joke, and something more than that: a joke that was necessary to her happiness and sanity as she went through the motions of being Walter's wife.

Leaving him was out of the question. Frank couldn't even support her decently, much less on the scale she was used to. And he wouldn't be able to support her at all if the man who owned the town conceived the notion that he should be fired. Walter was dim and slow, but Katy said he did have a vindictive streak. He remembered every unkind word that had ever been spoken to him, every blow he had ever accepted as a victim of schoolyard bullies.

Only once in his life, Katy said, had Walter ever taken an active hand in the running of his company. Shortly after inheriting it, he had relentlessly purged the mill's employment rolls of anyone who had ever given him offense. That done, he had retired to his basement with his toy trains.

Having accepted her reasons for playing it, Frank threw himself into the game with even more enthusiasm than Katy. He answered her questions about ballistics and fingerprints and all the other relatively unimportant details that civilians think about. But he reminded her that the perfect crime is the simplest. Alibis, locked rooms, exotic weapons, clever timetables, and theatrical disguises are the quickest paths to a conviction. And no matter how or where or when Walter was killed, she, as his wife and heir, would be the prime suspect.

"Since they're going to suspect you whatever you do, make it as simple as possible," he told her. "Shoot him down and say you thought he was a burglar, or you didn't know the gun was loaded. The put your faith in your money and a jury."

The game began to take up more and more of their time. Soon they hardly ever talked about anything else. And it began to impinge on their real lives. They both took extra precautions to avoid being seen together. They never repeated the mistake they had made the first time Katy visited him at his apartment, of leaving her car parked in front. But Frank told himself that these were simply the precautions that any sensible adulterers should take.

Frank supposed they played the game because any serious talk about their real future together would have been too depressing. They didn't have one.

Chapter Nine

Mario's Service Station was on the highway that touched the west end of town, just beyond the college campus. From the side street where Frank sat behind the wheel of Katy's parked car, he could see its lighted island clearly. The stickup man, if he scouted the area before hitting the gas station, would see Frank and Katy, too; but Frank believed he would take no notice of a couple in a parked car. It was stretching the rules, though.

". . . a perfect example of being too clever," he was saying. "If he gets electrocuted by his train set, they'll know it was murder. You have to shoot him."

"But I couldn't shoot him. You'd have to do it."

"Thanks. That's just the kind of complication that would hang us, if they still hanged people."

"I couldn't shoot him."

"We haven't even decided whether he's going to be shot. We have to use the means at hand. Does he have a gun?"

"Yes, a revolver."

"He's really making this tough for us. It's much easier to shoot yourself by accident with an automatic.

Why does he have it? Burglars, target shooting –"

"He uses it for playing Alan Ladd."

"Huh?"

"Well, when he has a few drinks, which isn't all that often, he'll take it out and stick it through his belt or put it in his pocket and pretend he's Alan Ladd in *This Gun for Hire.* He's crazy about old movies. He likes to watch gangster movies with the gun in his hand. He pretends to shoot at the commercials."

"I think we've got something here. Does he ever point it at you?"

"Sometimes."

"At himself?"

"Yes, a lot. He'll say something like, 'Want to see my Adolf Hitler imitation?' and he'll point the gun at his head and pull the trigger. He varies it. Sometimes he'll say it's his impression of Ernest Hemingway. Or he'll say, 'Hey, hon, I just thought of a great ending for one of those Russian plays,' and he'll pull the gun out of his pocket and put it to his temple."

"I'm not a psychiatrist, but I've been exposed to a lot of abnormal psychology in theory and practice," Frank said. "And it seems to me, if you just get him drunk often enough, he'll save us the trouble."

"I've thought that myself," she said seriously. "Inside, he's so small and dried-up . . . and he knows it. He's not a happy man. He's never gotten into the habit of being happy. He spent years under his crazy father's thumb; and all he learned to do was bitch and moan about it. I mistook that for sincerity and sensitivity. But he's sensitive the way a clam is sensitive, it shrinks when you squirt it with lemon juice."

"Well, all that isn't putting him out of his misery. We've got the gun, we've got the habit of playing with it – this is important: has anybody but you ever seen this act?"

She shrugged. "No – yes, the maid did once, Mrs. Ganley. He stayed home from the office one afternoon to watch one of his favorites. Christ, I even remember! It was Cape Fear with Robert Mitchum; he's crazy about that one. She came to tell me that Mr. Burroughs was sitting drunk in his study with a gun in his lap, talking to himself. And I told her that he does that sometimes, and that the gun was never loaded."

"That's perfect. That's almost too good," Frank said, laughing.

"What is?"

"What you told the maid. When she repeats it in court, it might sound like you were setting him up."

"It was – oh, it was two years ago."

"That's better. Anybody else? Anybody who's observed this habit?"

"Well, I've told people – Suzy Decker, for instance, and Quentin Swift –"

"They don't count. We need people who saw it."

"Yes. Yes, there were. Jay Rosenstein, his public relations man, and his wife. They were nice people, really unaffected and natural, not trying to suck up to Walter because he's the boss, and he sensed it. He was able to have a good time in company for once. Jay was even interested in his trains, and that made Walter his buddy for life. But Jay drinks a lot, and he's one of those people who can drink a lot without any apparent effect. Walter takes two drinks and becomes an entirely different person. Walter brought out the cognac after dinner, and nobody thought to put it away. Around ten o'clock, Walter staggered out of the room and came back with his gun. He said he thought that the Rosensteins, being Jewish, would appreciate his Adolf Hitler impression. I don't think he could have brought the evening to a more disastrous conclusion if he'd pulled down his pants and shit on the rug. Jay was really concerned, and he tried to take the gun away from Walter. Walter sort of danced around the table singing crazy things, like 'My gun is my fun, isn't it, hon?' and clicking the gun at us and himself. 'They all go on the run when Wally gets his gun,' he sang, and nobody ever called him *Wally* in his life. Jay told me he'd been in Vietnam, and he'd seen as many people get killed fooling around like this as any other way."

"Was he sober enough – Jay, I mean – to remember all this?"

"Oh, yes. I saw him at a cocktail party a few months later and we talked about it." She pondered for a moment. "Jay suggested obliquely – I guess you have to be oblique when you're talking to the boss's wife – that maybe it wouldn't hurt Walter to see a psychiatrist."

"On the basis of all this, I don't think it would be out of place for you to think about what you're going to wear in mourning," Frank said. "Walter is as good as snuffed."

"But it's only a game," she said sadly.

"Yes, it's only a game," he agreed.

"Look." She pointed toward the lighted island, where the kid on duty was waving frantically in their direction. "Do you suppose he wants you?"

"Shit," Frank said. "That's what I suppose he wants. I think I'll try to make myself more inconspicuous in the future by wearing a uniform and keeping a flashing red light on the car." He got out and shut the door behind him. "There's no point in your hanging around."

"I don't mind hanging around. I'll even come and hide under the counter with you, if you'd prefer."

"Won't your husband get nervous? – It's almost eleven."

"He thinks I went to the City Council meeting.

They're taking up a library appropriation tonight. And they go on till all hours; he's used to it."

"Well . . ."

"He's still waving, Frank. Maybe he was held up while we were plotting to murder Walter."

Frank laughed, even though her words didn't amuse him at all. He turned and trotted across the highway toward the attendant.

"You got a call," the kid said. "Some cop. Says it's important."

"Did he say who?"

"I don't know, some cop," the attendant said, turning his back. He was seldom civil. From little things he had observed since being here, he suspected that his stakeout was interfering with some profitable sideline the kid had going, like dealing in drugs or stolen auto parts.

He went to the phone in, the office. "Sgt. Buchanan," he said:

"Patrolman Elkins reporting, sergeant."

"You've got something to report?" It was the first time since the surveillance had begun that Ronnie had used this number.

"Yeah, shit, yeah, all kinds of stuff."

Frank sat down, shaking his jacket to unglue it from his back. It was a still, muggy night. He took awhile before speaking because he had resolved to be kind and patient at all times with Ronnie, who was, after all, doing him a big favor.

"Well, take it from the beginning, Ron."

"Let me take a look here in my notebook. I arrived at eight-thirty, just as Sonny Corcoran was leaving the house. He was wearing a suit and necktie. I was waiting to give him a couple blocks' lead before commencing to tail him, like you said, when a young male Caucasian who had been hiding in the shrubbery in front of the

Corcoran house came out and rang their bell. Ma opened the door and then slammed it in his face. He knocked. She opened it again, and they argued. At least, she did. She yelled at him a lot, but I couldn't make out what she was saying. Then she opened the screen door and let him in. You told me my duties were to tail Sonny and to observe anything out of the ordinary at the house, right?" When Frank said nothing, Ronnie repeated: "Right?"

"Yeah," Frank said, "that's what I told you."

"Okay, I wanted to get that straight, because when I finished observing this out-of-the-ordinary stuff at the house, Sonny was long gone. I went back to my car and boxed the area for a couple of blocks, but I couldn't find him. So I went back to the house and hid in the bushes where this young male Caucasian had been hiding."

Ronnie stopped. Frank supposed he was waiting for approval of his action. It seemed in order. In a suit and tie, Sonny was probably heading for a meeting of some civic improvement group. And, on his own, he was less of a threat than he would have been with Ma.

"You did just fine, Ronnie. That was the smart thing to do," Frank said.

"Yeah, as it turned out, it was. I was waiting in the bushes maybe ten minutes when Ma starts to screech her head off.f 'Rape!' she yells, 'Police!' little knowing that there was a police officer right on her own front stoop. I took out my piece and broke down the door, which turned out to be unlocked anyway. Ma was still screaming. I ran upstairs and apprehended the perpetrator in the act of trying to pull his pants on. Ma's clothing was torn, and she had a cut lip. She said the perpetrator hit her with a wrench that he had in his back pocket."

"Oh, for Christ's sake," Frank groaned.

"Huh?"

"Nothing, Ron, you did just fine. What did you do then?"

"I took them down to headquarters, and booked the perpetrator for attempted rape. Ma said he didn't actually stick it in, thanks to me getting there in time. She made a statement, and Dr. Goodwin came to examine her. Capt. LaPlante came to interrogate the guy, and he let me help for awhile. He thinks he might be the Full Moon Maniac. He said I'd probably get a citation, even if he isn't." Ronnie hesitated, then said in a halting voice: "Thank you, sergeant."

"You're welcome. What became of Ma?"

"Well, she took off while I was in the interrogation room. Should I of tailed her? I mean, wasn't that enough for one night?"

"That was plenty."

"One funny thing I almost forgot, this guy said you put him up to it. Going to see Ma, I mean, not trying to rape her. He said he didn't do that, of course, but what do you expect him to say?" Ronnie laughed.

"When did he say this?"

"Well, he started saying it in the car on the way to headquarters."

"Ma heard it?"

"Oh, yeah, she was right there in the front seat. He told the captain, too, but then he went on telling some crazy story about how some woman in a ski mask made him give her head. I don't think the captain believed him. I know I didn't."

"Good for you. What did he say happened at Ma's house?"

"Oh. He said Ma invited him upstairs to the bedroom and told him to take his clothes off. She waited till he did, then she went and took a look out the front window and started screaming and tearing her clothes.

He said she hit herself in the mouth with an ashtray. According to Ma, he chased her up the stairs and cornered her in the bedroom, where he hit her with the wrench."

"Sounds like you made a real good collar, Ron."

"That's what the captain said."

"You didn't tell the captain you were working for me; did you?"

"Oh, no. That's still top secret, right?"

"Right. And I want to make sure you get all the credit for this. Pulling me into it would only confuse people."

"Yeah, I'm kind of confused, myself. You want me to continue the surveillance, or maybe do something else for you?"

"I don't know. I'll talk to you tomorrow. And congratulations on a brilliant piece of police work."

"Thank you, sergeant," Ronnie said as Frank hung up.

Outside, the attendant was listlessly polishing one of the pumps. "How much longer you figure they'll keep you here?" he asked.

"If it works like usual, they'll pull me off the night before you get shot," Frank said coldly.

Back in the car, he found himself pouring out the whole mess to Katy. He hadn't done that in a long time. He'd used to tell his ex-wife about the disappointments and defeats he'd suffered on the job, but he'd learned to bottle it up when he'd seen that she wasn't interested. Now he couldn't seem to stop. He didn't minimize his own stupidity. He should have realized that an old hand like Ma would make Ronnie the minute he started hanging around Division Street; but, at the time, Ronnie's surveillance had seemed better than none at all. Aiming the oversexed Steve LaRue at her had been an even worse blunder. He hadn't needed Steve's probably useless identification to know that Ma was the one.

"How did she make Steve?" Katy asked, falling easily into his slang.

"That wasn't hard. First she sees Ronnie moping around, and then the only possible witness against her shows up at the front door. And the jerk took a wrench with him; because he was afraid of Sonny. You don't stay in the whorehouse business for long; even an amateur operation like Ma used to run, unless you can spot a wrench in a guy's pocket at fifty paces. He set himself up."

"No, you set him up," she said firmly. "Ronnie's getting a medal out of this, but Steve's in jail. What are you going, to do about it?"

"He'll be out tomorrow morning, whatever I do. But I'll tell him I'll pull some strings if he keeps his mouth shut. The prosecutor won't touch this one. Raping Ma Corcoran, that's like stealing a religious handbill from a dedicated evangelist."

"You're pretty unscrupulous, aren't you," she stated. "Why won't you murder my husband?"

"That's different."

She thought for a moment. "Remember when you were trying to hand me that line of bullshit about what civilization is all about?"

"I told you, it wasn't entirely bullshit."

"The better I know you, the more I'm inclined to think it was. But one of the things it's all about, really, is making sure that none of us has to go up against pure evil on our own. Ma Corcoran is pure evil. If you keep trying to get her all by yourself, she'll destroy you. She already knows who sent Steve after her. She knows you beat up Sonny. She's probably figured out why Ronnie was watching her."

"I'm not trying to fight pure evil," he said. "I'm just trying to get promoted over the captain."

"Something's going on over there," she said urgently, pointing through the windshield.

"Oh, yes. Excuse me."

He jumped out of the car and sprinted across the highway. The Magnum from his shoulder-holster was out and extended in both hands when he skidded to a stop at the office door.

"Police officer!" he shouted. "Freeze!"

The man in the windbreaker and stocking-mask who was holding the attendant at gunpoint jerked his head around. Frank started to squeeze the trigger.

"Don't shoot, Filthy Frank, you got me!" the man said, letting his gun drop, to the floor. "Please, don't shoot!"

Frank eased the pressure on the trigger. This was the second time in recent weeks that someone had called him that, Sonny having been the first, and it puzzled him. He didn't like it, either. He supposed it was a perverse reference to his habitual neatness. In the twisted world of these scumbags, cleanliness was filth.

"I guess you won't have to hang around anymore now, huh?" the attendant asked as Frank cuffed the stickup man.

"I've grown very fond of this place," Frank said as he tossed the suspect. He came up with a second gun taped to his ankle. "Maybe I'll keep hanging around. I hear someone in the neighborhood is dealing dope to the college kids."

The kid's eyes flickered away nervously.

Frank turned the prisoner around and tore off the stocking mask. He was a large black in his twenties, and he was soaked with the sweat of fear. Frank pushed the muzzle of his gun up under his jaw, forcing him to stand on tiptoe.

"I must advise you that you have the absolute right to remain silent. You also have the right to have an attorney present at all times. If you cannot afford an attorney, one will be provided for you. Do you understand what I've just told you?"

"Yes, sir."

"Did you hear me tell him that?" Frank asked the attendant.

"Yes, sir," the attendant said.

"Okay. If you pull any of those Mickey Mouse rights on me, scumbag," Frank said, cocking his piece and shoving it up harder under the mart's jaw, "I will blow your motherfucking head off. Now, tell me your full name and address, and tell me all about the last five places you knocked over."

After the long recitation was finished, Frank put his gun away and patted the man on the shoulder amiably. He turned to the attendant. "You heard all that, didn't you? How I gave him his rights and he made a statement of his own free will?"

"Yeah."

"Well, don't forget it, and maybe I won't need to come back."

"No wonder – never mind," the attendant said. "I won't forget."

"Honky motherfuckers!" the black man spat. "You all in it together to screw the black man out of his rights!"

"That's right. That's exactly how it works," Frank said, kicking him off his feet and making him crash to the floor as he walked to the telephone.

Out on the apron, waiting with his prisoner and his witness for the patrol car he had summoned, he waved Katy away. She honked in return: ten beeps that he recognized as an attempt to render, in monotone, the opening of the last movement of Mozart's Jupiter Symphony. The attendant turned to look, but Frank was certain that he wasn't able, at this distance and in this light, to identify the make or model of her car.

At headquarters, Capt. LaPlante, rumpled and red-eyed, clapped him on the shoulder.

"That was a good collar, Frank. A fine piece of police work."

"Thank you, captain."

"We've got a kid downstairs named. Steve LaRue who's been telling us a funny story –"

"Oh, yeah, him. He's been a little crazy since his girl friend got raped. He came to me the other day with a story about how he got raped, too." Frank laughed. "He told me his assailant looked like Racquel Welch, and then he said he thought it was Ma Corcoran."

"Yeah," LaPlante said thoughtfully. "That's pretty much . . . he came to you, huh? Why didn't you tell me about it?"

"Maybe I did wrong, but I figured you got enough screwballs on your back."

"Well, yeah. But we can't discount any possibility. Next time, tell me, okay?"

Frank breathed only a little more easily. Maybe he had diverted the captain for the moment, but he knew that LaPlante liked to go over the same ground more than once. He might come back and dig up this bone tomorrow or the next day and chew on it some more.

"You figure you'll check out Ma?" Frank asked casually.

"Hell, no. Even this charge we have him on – I figure she set him up, it's some kind of neighborhood squabble. Maybe he's been pissing on Sonny's flowers."

The captain turned to say something to the desk sergeant, but Frank interrupted him: "I've got a line on the French Club knifing. I think I can make an arrest tomorrow."

"Well, that's fine. It's good to see somebody getting results around here. I'm sure as hell not."

"So I was wondering, maybe I could go back to work with you on the Maniac investigation."

LaPlante hesitated, then said: "I don't know. I'll talk to you tomorrow." As Frank left, the captain called after him: "Congratulations on a fine piece of police work."

Driving home, Frank reflected that "LaPlante" probably meant "the vegetable" in French.

Nobody had ever tried to assassinate Frank, but he wouldn't have been willing to lay odds that nobody ever would. When he arrived home to find a strange car parked in the garage beneath his apartment, he backed out of the driveway fast. He drew the Magnum before getting out of his car. Then he drew the .38 from the clamshell holster on his belt.

He approached the garage warily, trying to watch the car and the dark shrubbery around him at the same time. The car was a dark-blue Stingray. He noted a college faculty parking sticker on the rear bumper. He relaxed slightly. Some drunk from the college had considered his garage a good place to park and sleep it off that seemed a more likely explanation than his first thought.

He poked a gun barrel around the corner of the garage door to snap on the lights, quickly dropping to his knee and covering the car.

"Police officer!" he shouted. "Come out of that car with your hands up!"

A dog began barking down the street. A light came on in the main house, his landlord's. Gleaming in the flat light of the overhead bulb, the lifeless car somehow radiated menace.

He got to his feet cautiously and moved forward. He saw a tangle of naked bodies inside the car. He jerked the door open. The man and the woman didn't. move, and he saw that they weren't going to.

The Maniac was still taking souvenirs but had graduated from shoes and bras and panties. This time he'd taken their heads.

Chapter Ten

Two police cars, one of them unmarked, pulled up in front of Suzy Decker's house in the morning. Capt. LaPlante and a uniformed policeman entered the house, using a key. Ronnie Elkins waited at the wheel of the black-and-white. Raymond Corcoran walked across the street to question him.

"Hello, Sonny," Ronnie said. "I thought you were working these days."

"I stayed home to take care of Ma, after what happened last night. You did real good."

"It's what they pay me for," Ronnie said modestly.

"What's the matter here?" Raymond asked, gesturing toward the house.

"Somebody wasted the cunt that lived here. First he cornholed her, then he cut off her head with a chain saw. And then –" Ronnie had to struggle to get his laughter under control – "and then he dumped the bodies, her and her boyfriend, in Filthy Frank's garage. How about that?"

"Mrs. Decker was a friend of mine," Raymond said gravely.

"Maybe you better tell that to the captain. Yeah, I

think you better."

"Who was the man?"

"A professor from the college named Swift."

"I heard of him."

"You did? How?"

"I don't remember."

"Maybe the captain can help you. You better go on inside, Sonny," Ronnie said, getting out of the car and guiding him in the direction of the house.

All the cops called him "Sonny," but Raymond didn't like it. He had acquired the nickname in the first place because Ma's boyfriends had never bothered to remember his real name: "Go out and play, Sonny"; "Get lost, Sonny." He used to tolerate it from the cops because they used to be his friends, but lately they hadn't been friendly.

Outside, Suzy Decker's house was just another drab bungalow. Inside, it jangled with vivid colors and glittering surfaces. She had no ordinary furniture in the living room, just giant pillows arranged as the whim struck her. Whenever Raymond had eaten here, she'd brought out a table with no legs and made him sit on the floor. That was how the Japanese did it, she'd said.

Capt. LaPlante was seated at her desk in an alcove between the kitchen and the main room. He was looking through her correspondence, mostly bills.

"This is Sonny Corcoran, Captain," Ronnie said. "He said he was a friend of the deceased."

"I know Sonny. How are you, kid?"

"One of Sonny's sidelines is cutting firewood;" Ronnie added quickly, "with a chainsaw."

"That'll be all, Elkins."

"Yes, sir." Ronnie left.

"I didn't kill Mrs. Decker," Sonny said.

"Nobody said you did."

"He just did, more or less. He's been following me around for the past week. Is that why, because you think I'm doing all those things?"

"Was he following you last night?"

"No, I guess not. That was when that guy tried to hurt Ma."

"Where were you at the time?"

"I was at the City Council meeting. They were supposed to discuss the traffic light that we want on the corner of Division Street and Railroad Avenue, where the kid got run over last month. I had a speech wrote – *written* – down that I wanted to say. I got there late, but I stayed till it ended, because the traffic light was the last thing they talked about. That was after one o'clock."

"What time did you get there?"

"About nine. There were no seats left in back so I had to go up and sit in the front row."

LaPlante snorted. "That sounds like a pretty good alibi."

"It isn't an alibi, it's where I was."

"Okay, calm down. That's all the word means, that you were someplace else. How well did you know this woman?"

"Pretty well. I mowed her lawn for her."

"Aren't you kind of old for that work?"

Sonny jerked as if he'd touched a snake. Unnoticed during the exchange, Frank Buchanan had entered the room and was watching him alertly.

"What's the matter?" LaPlante said.

"Nothing. She didn't pay me to mow it. Somebody had to do it."

"So you were a good friend of hers, huh? Did her favors like that?"

"He was fucking her," Frank said, "until she ditched him for the professor. Right, Sonny?"

"Do I have to listen to that kind of dirty talk, captain? It would be bad enough even if she wasn't dead."

"Just answer the question, Sonny," LaPlante said.

"It wasn't like that. I hadn't seen her for about a month, that's all. I didn't know about any professor. She wasn't very nice, sometimes, so I stopped coming around. She didn't ditch me."

"Why wasn't she nice?" LaPlante asked.

"I would tell her important things, and she'd pretend to listen, but I could see she was laughing at me. I could see she thought I wasn't very smart."

"So you cut off her head with your chainsaw," Frank said.

Raymond stood silent, fighting against the urge to walk over to Frank and smash him. Frank had beaten him up once, but he'd started by hitting him from behind and he'd finished the job with a lead-weighted sap. But Ravmond was bigger and stronger. He knew that he could beat Frank if he could get a good grip on him.

"Where do you keep your chainsaw, Sonny?" the captain asked.

"It's not mine, it's Ma's."

"She's going to be mad at you, cutting up people without her permission," Frank said. "Or was she with you?"

The uniformed policeman who had been standing, unspeaking, beside LaPlante now drew his nightstick and moved closer to Raymond. Instead of rushing at Frank, as he wanted to, Raymond turned to the captain.

"Let me talk to you alone, captain. This guy gets me mad, and when I get mad I can't think too good."

"You have something to say to me alone, Sonny?"

"No. Of course not. That's what I mean."

"You can't get confused if you tell us the truth," the captain said, standing up. "Where does your Ma keep her chainsaw?"

"In the back of the Land Rover. We ain't used it – *haven't* used it – since last year."

"She home?"

"Yes."

"Well, let's go talk to her," the captain said, guiding him by the arm. Frank stood in their way.

"I'd like to keep him here and ask him a couple more questions, captain, if that's okay with you."

LaPlante shrugged. "Suit yourself. See if you can find anything here. There was nothing in the desk. Maybe she keeps her trick-book in the bedroom."

"She wasn't like that!" Raymond protested.

LaPlante ignored him. "I'll be at headquarters when I finish with Ma. You want Donovan – ?"

"Leave Elkins, would you? He knows this guy," Frank said.

"I'm sure their conversation would be inspiring," the captain said as he walked out with the patrolman.

"Ronnie!" Frank called from the door.

"Hey, captain!" Raymond shouted. "Don't leave me here with Filthy Frank!"

LaPlante didn't look back.

"Why do you call me that, Sonny?" Frank asked pleasantly.

"Everybody calls you that."

"I don't like it."

"Fuck you," Sonny said, and Frank kneed him in the groin before he had finished speaking. He fell to the floor, struggling for breath, but his lungs seemed paralyzed by the pain.

"Close the door after you, Ron," Frank said. "We're going to get together for another brilliant piece of police work."

"What's the matter with him?" Ronnie asked.

"Nothing at all, compared to what's going to be the matter with him. Cuff him to the radiator."

Raymond tried to resist. He could have taken Ronnie Elkins even more easily than Frank Buchanan, but he couldn't even stand yet. Ronnie dragged him across the floor and handcuffed him behind his back, passing the chain through a coil of the radiator.

"Now stuff his shirt in his mouth," Frank said.

Ronnie looked puzzled for a moment, but then he ripped Raymond's T-shirt down the front and tore it off his shoulders.

"He won't open his mouth," Ronnie said.

"If you hold his nose long enough, he will," Frank said.

Unable to twist away from Ronnie's pinching grip, Raymond at last opened his mouth to gulp for air and shout: "Cap –" Bonnie rammed the wadded T-shirt in before he could finish.

"What now?" Bonnie asked.

"Take off your belt, wrap it around your hand, and beat the shit out of him," Frank said, standing by the window and moving the drape aside slightly as he peered down the street.

Ronnie laughed. "I'm not supposed to do stuff like that." He was silent for a moment. "Am I?" Then he added, "Why?"

"Because Sonny and his mother are the Full Moon Maniac. That's why I had you watching them. That didn't work too well, and it gave them such a laugh that they decided to rub it in by dumping their shit on my doorstep. So now we're going to bounce Sonny off the walls until he tells us what we want to hear."

"Oh. How can he tell us with a gag in his mouth?"

"That's just until the captain leaves," Frank said. "Try not to hit him too much in the face. Tell me when you get tired, and I'll spell you."

Raymond screamed into his gag as Ronnie wrapped his belt around his hand, but he knew that the sound didn't carry beyond the room. He pulled his knees tight against his chest and lowered his head, but Ronnie kicked him in the shins with alternate feet until he was forced to roll away. Then Ronnie kicked him in the back. As he rolled over again, tearing his wrists in an effort to break the handcuffs, the policeman knelt over him and punched him repeatedly in the stomach. He saw that Frank wasn't even watching, but kept staring out the window around the corner of the drape.

When Ronnie stood up, panting, Raymond kicked him in his protuberant belly with both feet. Ronnie let out a "whoosh" of breath and sat down so hard that the house shook.

"Fucking bastard!" Ronnie gasped, driving his bound fist into Raymond's mouth and banging his head against the radiator.

"Watch the face," Frank said mildly. "And take off those shades."

Ronnie pulled off Raymond's glasses, flung them to floor, and ground them under his heel. Raymond blinked against the light, which had always hurt his eyes. That pain seemed unimportant now.

"Looks like a fucking mole, don't he?" Bonnie giggled.

Frank studied him thoughtfully. "You know, I think he looks a lot like Walter Burroughs."

"Well, Walter Burroughs looks like a mole, too," Ronnie laughed. "That's why."

Raymond raged to hear his secret bandied about by these two. He could have killed them before, but now he wanted to do it in some terrible and appropriate way. Mrs. Burroughs, too, the whore, she must have told; they all must have laughed over it. He'd followed her a few times since their first meeting: once to Filthy Frank's place, where she'd spent the afternoon. It hurt him to know that his father was married to a woman no better than Gretchen Slovik, no better than Suzy Decker had been.

Concentrating hard on revenge – maybe he would lie in wait for them with Ma's chainsaw – he hardly noticed Ronnie's next few blows. Noting his inattention, Ronnie kicked him in the balls. He threw up into the gag and began to strangle on his vomit.

"Take the gag out," Frank said. "And be careful of your . . . uniform."

"Shit!" Ronnie screamed, as Frank's warning had come to late. He slammed Raymond's head back and forth, spraying blood and vomit around the room's bright cushions. "Shit!"

"I said, watch his face," Frank cautioned.

"Captain! Captain LaPlante!" Raymond shouted.

"Save your breath. He's gone. He took your chainsaw with him, but I figure you and Ma spent the morning taking it apart and scrubbing down the pieces with carbolic acid. If they find any traces of blood, you'll both swear that Ma cut herself on it last year," Frank said.

Raymond glared at him, wondering how he knew all that. "She did," he said. "She cut her arm on it last winter."

"That's a goddamned lie," Frank said, "but I'll let you get away with one. Keep in mind that I wanted to catch you in the act, Sonny, so I could shoot you down like a mad dog. I'm disappointed that I can't do that. Maybe I'll do it anyway; if I don't like your answers. How many girls have you raped altogether?"

"Nobody."

Frank nodded to Ronnie, who looked puzzled, so Frank said. "Hit him."

Ronnie kicked him in the belly. While Raymond was still doubled up and retching dryly, Frank said, "We'll start with the one the juvenile authorities know about, Geraldine Francis."

"I didn't rape her! She wanted me to show her my thing. She was playing with it when her mother walked in on us, so she said I made her do it."

"Yeah, at the age of fourteen you were molested by a twelve-year-old girl. The juvenile court didn't buy that, either. Do him again Ron."

Ronnie hit him in the mouth with his fist. Raymond felt his teeth crack.

"How many?"

Raymond shook his head. He was soaking wet. He saw that Ronnie held a wet pot from the kitchen. He must have been unconscious for a time. It was hard to make his swollen, aching lips form the word: "What?"

"How many girls have you raped? I figure ten or twelve."

"We could, heat up a pan on the kitchen stove and put it to his feet," Ronnie suggested.

"Don't get creative, Ron. And don't hit him in the face anymore. Just hit him."

Raymond tried to curl into a ball again, forgetting that the small of his back was fearfully vulnerable. Ronnie kicked him there.

"How many?" Frank asked.

"Whatever you say."

"No, it's what you say. You have to tell me the truth."

Raymond felt sick and dizzy, but that in no way minimized the pain. Every square inch of his body hurt. There was no part he could have offered for the next blow. If he told them what they wanted to know, it would end. He wished he had told Ma where he was going. She was just down the street. She would have stopped them.

"Ten," he said.

"Very good! When did you start?"

"Like you said, with Geraldine."

"When did you start as the Full Moon Maniac?"

"I don't know, two years ago."

"Did you start on your own, or did Ma put you up to it from the beginning?"

"Ma never knew about it. I –"

He missed Frank's signal, because Ronnie's kick to his stomach came as a surprise.

"She made me do it," he gasped. "It was her idea from the start."

"Why?"

"She wanted to watch."

"Who was the first?"

"Some girl who came around selling magazines, a college girl. Ma told me to take off her clothes and do things to her. Then Ma made her do things."

"Like what?"

"You know, like kissing her between the legs and all. Ma said she wouldn't tell because she was too stuck-up. It would embarrass her too much. I guess she didn't. I thought she was real nice; I was sorry I made her cry."

This time, Frank kicked him.

"What did you do that for? I'm telling! I'm telling you the truth!"

"You got to remember, Sonny, I enjoy kicking you. Sometimes I just do it for fun. If you keep talking, maybe you'll hold my interest and make me forget how much I like it. So who was next? Did you start going up in the woods then?"

"Yeah, that's when we started. It was some couple, I don't know who. And then another one, and another one after that."

"You know who they were. You read the papers, Sonny."

"I don't read the nasty stuff. It's disgusting, the stuff they put in the papers."

Ronnie laughed loudly.

"You must've recognized some of them. You knew Steve LaRue, for instance."

"Yeah, him."

"Was he the only one Ma showed herself to?"

"Yeah; I guess." He saw Frank start to look in Ronnie's direction, so he cried hastily: "Yes, yes! He was the only one. The other times she just watched."

"What about the Evans kid, the first one who got shot? Didn't she make him screw her? And then she shot him?"

"Yeah, that's right. I forgot. Only I shot him."

"What with?"

"A gun – no, don't hit me again, please don't! I thought that was the answer, honest!"

"What did you do with the gun?"

"After I shot him, I threw it into the river. Off the Water Street bridge."

"You're lying," Frank said, and this time Frank hit him in the face.

"What did I say wrong? What was I supposed to say?"

"The same gun killed Boisvert and Oates, six months later."

"Well, that's when I threw it in. You got me confused. I can't think. I shot them, too."

"Who lit the match?"

"What match?"

Frank motioned Ronnie to strike. Raymond felt nothing. Then Ronnie was again standing over him with the dripping pot.

"Somebody set fire to their car. I figure Ma did it."

Raymond didn't want to implicate Ma too seriously, but he wanted to please Frank at any cost. Setting fire to a car didn't sound all that bad. "Yeah, she did that."

He added: "She dropped a cigarette into the gas tank."

"Brave girl," Frank said. "It's a shame she didn't blow herself up. What did you do with all the souvenirs?"

"I don't know what you mean – no, I don't, really! Tell me what you mean, I'll talk!"

"Bras, panties, all that shit you took from the victims. Where is it?"

"Oh, Ma took that. I guess she's got it in her room someplace."

Frank looked at him oddly, but he let the answer pass. "Tell me about last night," he said. "What was that shit you were feeding LaPlante about the City Council meeting?"

"They made all the people leave the room at about ten o'clock. That's what they call an executive session," Raymond explained. "I slipped out then, and Ma was waiting for me. We did what we did, and then I snuck back into the meeting around midnight. Nobody noticed me, and then I stood up and said something when they came to the traffic light."

"Ma must have had them spotted."

Raymond nodded. "She drove me right to them. They were parked by the college. I got out and pointed a gun at them."

"The same one you keep throwing in the river?"

"No, no, a different one. Ma's. A sawed-off shotgun."

"They're illegal," Ronnie said sternly.

"I didn't know that," Sonny said earnestly. "I tied them up and made them get into the trunk of our car."

"The Pinto?" Frank asked incredulously.

"No, no, I don't mean the trunk, it was the Land Rover. I put them in the back and put a blanket over them. I drove their car. We went down in back of the old railroad yards, near the mill."

"What did you do then?"

"I did things to her, you know."

"Exactly what things?"

Raymond flicked a nervous glance at Ronnie. "I cornholed her."

"I'm surprised to hear you use a naughty word like that, Sonny," Frank said, and he slapped him hard across the face. "Tell me in proper language."

Raymond hesitated. Then Ronnie growled, "You mean you screwed her up the ass, you rotten pervert," and he kicked him in the stomach.

"Yes, yes, that's what I did!" Raymond gasped. "And then I cut their heads off with the chainsaw and we took them to your place."

"What did you do with them? The heads?"

"I threw them off the bridge. In a bag, a burlap bag with rocks in it."

Frank sat down on one of the big cushions and chewed his lip for a while. Ronnie watched him alertly, as if waiting for another signal. Sonny concentrated on trying to breathe without hurting his chest.

"Okay, Sonny, listen carefully. I must advise you that you have the absolute right to remain silent. You also have the right to have an attorney present at all times. If you cannot afford an attorney, one will be provided for you. Do you understand what I've just told you?"

"Does that mean I can see a lawyer?"

Frank waved a weary hand at Ronnie, who kicked him again.

"It means you have to say 'Yes' to the question I just asked you, that's all it means."

"Yes," Raymond groaned.

"You heard that, Ron?"

"Yeah, sergeant," Ronnie laughed. "That makes it all legal, huh?"

"You bet your ass it does. It's a shame we made such a fucking mess out of him. We'll have to get him downtown fast and take some pictures before he blows up like a balloon. What happened is this: after I gave him his rights and he made his voluntary statement, he tried to make a break for it. He's a very strong kid. We had to use a lot of necessary force – remember those words, Ronnie, we used only *the force that was necessary* to subdue him."

"Necessary force," Ronnie repeated. "Yeah, I know that one, sergeant."

"Good for you. You'll get a gold shield next week, if I have anything to say about it. Get some ice from the kitchen, put it in a towel, and hold it to his face, especially around the eyes and mouth, while I type up a statement for him on his old girl friend's typewriter."

"What's a gold shield?"

"It's what you get for brilliant police work, Ron. You've done it again."

Ronnie glowed, standing taller as he strode to the kitchen.

Chapter Eleven

Armed with the confession, Frank was able to override LaPlante's bewilderment and hustle him into endorsing his request for a warrant for Ma Corcoran's arrest and a warrant to search her house.

Four hours after securing the warrants, he was still searching the house without success when the phone rang.

"Hello?"

"Stop, Frank." It was LaPlante.

"What, the search? We've already turned up an illegal arsenal, six ounces of marijuana, some pornographic films involving minors –"

"Put them all back, nice and neat, and just hope that Ma doesn't sue you for wrecking her house, on top of everything else you're going to get sued for."

"You're crazy."

"I'd take issue with that if you were still an active member of this department, but you're not. Maybe you've forgotten, but if you falsify your probable cause for a warrant, then your warrant is no good, and anything you find is worthless."

"Sonny's confession –"

The captain interrupted with a humorless laugh. "I'd say that the confession is worthless, too, except that it's going to be the main piece of evidence in the various criminal and civil proceedings against you and me and the department."

"What's wrong with it?"

"Come off it, Frank! You beat it out of him, and there's not a word of truth in it. Sonny's got a few witnesses to the fact that he never left the City Council meeting last night, including Chief Hoskins, the mayor, and three newspaper reporters."

"The executive session –"

"They didn't hold one. He sat in the front row, next to Chief Hoskins, all night."

"Where was Ma?"

LaPlante sighed. "She was touching none other than Walter Burroughs for a loan. It seems he holds the mortgage on her house; they've done business before, so there was a lot of paperwork to go over. He backs her up."

"For Christ's sake, that's Sonny's father! He'd say –"

"Frank, Frank," LaPlante cut in. "Haven't you got enough trouble, without a slander suit from Mr. Walter Burroughs?" He paused for a moment, then said: "Let's see where else your airtight case breaks down. Oh, yeah. No blood on the chainsaw. Sonny has an alibi from Gretchen Slovik for the night of the last killings."

"What about Ma's alibi?"

"She doesn't need one. We're looking for a man, remember? I'm looking, I mean. You ought to be looking for a lawyer and a job."

"You still have Steve LaRue's story."

"No, we don't. Ma dropped the charge, and Steve retracted his story. He says he was under a terrible strain, mainly from you harassing him, which sounds like he might be getting in line to sue you, too. Not to be outdone, the lawyer for that coon you busted the other night is talking about going to Federal Court with a civil rights complaint."

"Okay, I get the picture. But when you find the Full Moon Maniac –"

"It'll probably turn out to be you," LaPlante said wearily. "You can turn in your shield and your service revolver at your convenience, provided that's within the next hour. And don't go anywhere. You'll have to answer some questions for a grand jury. Is Elkins still with you?"

"He's here. Is he suspended, too?"

"Yeah, only I want to tell him myself, so he doesn't do something dumb, like shoot you. Send him back to the barn."

Later that afternoon, at his apartment, he told his troubles to Katy.

"It's crazy," she said, after thinking for a while.

"Not at all. They have me cold. They have no choice but to suspend me."

She glared at him. "Not them, idiot! You! After fifteen years on the police force, don't you know any better than to pull this kind of dumb shit?"

He laughed. He didn't usually drink much, but now he was drinking gin over ice. He refilled his glass and held up the bottle, but she shook her head vigorously.

"I always got away with it before," he said. "Nothing quite this bad, that's true, but I've never before been so absolutely certain about someone I couldn't hang legally. Sonny did it. Ma did it. I don't have a shred of doubt in my mind."

"Maybe that's so. But all you've done is to prove that they're smarter than you are."

"I'll drink to that," he said. "That son-of-a-bitch is a hell of a lot smarter than I thought. He came up with a detailed confession. Only thing wrong with it, every detail was incorrect. He grabbed me right from the beginning with his story about the door-to-door salesgirl. I've never heard anything that sounded more like a straight confession. And then he led me right up the garden path. I figure Ma must have coached him on it, as their first line of defense, after she found out I was interested in him."

They stared at each other. They were both fully clothed. They hadn't made love. Neither of them wanted to. Frank wondered if the honeymoon was over. He laughed at his thought, and she frowned at him as if she could read it.

"But the City Council –"

"Oh, bullshit!" he shouted, slamming his glass down on the coffee table so hard that the liquor flew out. "None of them was sitting there watching Sonny all night. He was there toward the beginning, he was there at the end, that's all they know. It's too good, don't you see? It's all too good to be true: Dumping the bodies in my garage. Who else would do that? Some other suspect? We don't have one. I wasn't even assigned to the case. But I was leaning on Sonny on my own time."

She looked ill. It took him a moment to remember that the people he'd found in his garage had been friends of hers. Odd friends: a philandering professor and the sort of woman who would sleep with Sonny Corcoran. He realized that he was looking for an excuse to wound her, and the knowledge momentarily shamed him. He refilled his glass and made an effort to calm himself.

"Change of life," he said.

"What?"

"Middle-aged desperation. This case seemed like a big chance, probably the last chance I would ever get to break out of this rut. I was going to get promoted over the captain, then run for mayor, some such shit. And I hated these people, Sonny and Ma, like I've never hated the other scumbags I've gone against. Maybe I hated them because they were standing in my way. That's why I acted stupidly, to answer your original question."

"Drinking straight gin isn't going to help."

"Yes, it is. I have to perfect my act as a skid-row bum. Even the security guard's job I used to sneer at is beyond my reach. What they'll do is, they'll let Ronnie Elkins save his ass by spilling everything, and they'll convict me. I'll go to jail." He laughed until tears ran down his cheeks. "I'm going to fucking jail!"

"There must be something you can do."

"Sure, there is." He got up and paced. He stopped at the window and saw that night had fallen, unnoticed. "I can shoot Sonny and threaten to shoot Ronnie, and there go the witnesses: Only they'd know who did it, wouldn't they?"

"Seriously, I mean, there must be –"

"Oh, I'm serious. How do you suppose smart criminals get off? They kill or intimidate the witnesses; it happens all the time. I'm a criminal. I haven't been very smart up until now, but it's time I wised up, don't you think?"

"Sobered up, maybe. And I think it's time I went home." But she made no move to go.

"There is another alternative," he said.

"What?"

"We can snuff Walter."

"I don't feel like playing that tonight," she said, looking away.

"Who's playing?" He sat down at the table and tried to will her to meet his level gaze. She did and looked quickly away again. "Then we can buy the witnesses. Buy a lawyer, buy a jury, buy the fucking judge. Nobody has to die except the simple-minded cocksucker who gave Ma Corcoran an alibi while she was sawing off your friends' heads."

"Please –" She couldn't continue. All the color left her face, and he thought that he might have pushed too hard, but she recovered. "I don't know why he did it. Maybe because he thinks he's Sonny's father. And just maybe because he was telling the truth."

Frank's laugh was more like a bark.

"You said it yourself, more or less," she continued, "that you've lost your perspective on this case, that it's become an obsession. Ma Corcoran is a monster, okay, and her son is a half-wit, but it's just possible that they're innocent of these crimes. The only thing you've got that resembles evidence is Steve LaRue's story, and he's changed it. Maybe what he told you never happened. Maybe you were harassing him, and he told you something he thought you'd like to hear."

He sighed. "I don't care. I'm not a cop. They can rape and murder the entire population of Armitage; I don't give a shit about their guilt or innocence. What I was talking about was you and me snuffing Walter."

"I have to go," she said, getting up.

"Please don't go."

"It isn't much fun, watching you get drunk and feel sorry for yourself," she said, but she sat down.

"Save me from myself by having another drink," he said. He found that he could walk steadily to the daybed where she sat without significant effort. His hand was steady when he refilled her glass. She accepted it.

"It's summertime," he said, smiling easily. "Why aren't you at your summer house? Don't you have one, up at the lake?"

She seemed greatly relieved by the change of subject, by the change in his manner. "Being alone with Walter isn't all that attractive – this summer, especially," she added with a significant smile. "And he can't bear to part from his trains."

"But didn't you used to go?"

"Almost every year. We went last year, as a matter of fact, because I felt like loafing and swimming. He pretended he had to go to the office, so I was alone a lot. This year we rented it for the months of June and July, and the subject of going just never came up."

"I'm surprised you didn't inspect it after your tenants left. That's no way for rich folks to behave."

"Some real estate lady took care of it; I suppose we have her word it's in order. Are you trying to get rid of me?"

"Well, I've got lots of time on my hands now to swim and loaf. If Walter hung around the city, I could come visit you a lot."

"It would be the ideal place," she said thoughtfully. "We – Walter owns one whole end of the lake, so you can literally see anyone coming for a mile away, on the road that follows the south shore."

"No back way?"

"Just a footpath that leads to a back road. Walter wouldn't use it to surprise us. He'd be afraid of bears and wolves, or of getting lost."

"But I could use it, so I wouldn't advertise myself to everybody around the lake."

"Oh, yes. I suppose you could. But the summer's almost over, and that lake is like ice water even in the middle of July."

"Is there a telephone?"

"Yes, but I suppose it's disconnected. Tenants never forget to have that done. Why all these questions?"

He studied her in silence for a moment. He smiled. She returned his smile uncertainly.

"Let's say that you and Walter went up there for –

oh, for a week. To take advantage of the last nice weather. To check up on the tenants. To batten down the hatches for the winter. Would you bother to have the telephone connected for just that week?"

"We've done that sort of thing in the past. And no, we never bothered with the phone. Walter would always leave the number of the general store across the lake at the mill, and he'd made a show of giving the storekeeper twenty dollars to make sure his messages were relayed immediately. But nobody ever called him."

"I'll bet he has a television set up there," Frank said.

"Of course he does. Why are you asking me all these questions, Frank?"

"Because that's where we're going to snuff him."

"I told you, I don't feel like playing. I can't joke about murdering somebody . . ." She gestured vaguely at the floor, and at the garage beneath it.

"And I told you, I'm not joking. I thought Ma and Sonny were my last chance. But Walter is."

"Frank . . . I can get you a lawyer, the best lawyer I can buy. Maybe – no, no maybe about it, I can use Walter's influence to pressure people. I can tell him that I egged you on because I was so upset about Suzy, that I feel responsible for your problems. Walter would buy that story, and he'll do anything I ask him."

"Not if he thinks Sonny Corcoran is his flesh and blood."

"He'll *do* it for me, Frank, believe me! Why don't you stand up and fight? Fight to stay out of jail. Fight to keep your job. I'll help you."

"Screw the job. Do you think I want to be a cop for the rest of my life?" He laughed. "I want to be the pampered lapdog of a rich, beautiful widow."

That line had always made her laugh before, but this time she only smiled coldly. She stood up and slung her bag over her shoulder. "I believe you, Frank. I know you're telling me the truth. I understand that fighting isn't your style. Beating up kids in handcuffs, maybe, but not fighting."

He got up and walked to the rack where he kept his clothes. His course impeded her path to the stairs, and she waited impatiently for him to get out of the way. He didn't. He pulled his Colt Python from the holster hanging on the rack and checked the cylinder.

"I've lost everything, Katy, except you," he said. "Except this. If you leave now, I'll use it on myself."

"Bullshit!" she snapped, pushing past him. "Anyway, that's a woman's line."

He waited till the clatter of her footsteps had progressed halfway down the stairs. Then he raised the pistol to his shoulder and fired a round through the roof. She rushed back immediately, white-faced, wide-eyed.

"Oh, God!" she screamed. *"God!* Why can't I meet a *man* for once?"

"Try Ma Corcoran!" he shouted down the stairs after her. "You stupid cunt!"

Chapter Twelve

On Sunday afternoon, Walter drank sparingly as he watched *White Heat* in his study. Katy watched, too, in a desperate search for distraction, and she drank less sparingly.

"What bothers me about this film," Walter said during a commercial, "is that the hero is a fink. I mean, here you've got this powerful character, this regular dynamo played by Cagney, and you're supposed to be sympathizing with the police spy, Edmond O'Brien. It just doesn't work."

What bothered her about the movie was that it reminded her of the Corcorans. Cagney had a tough old bitch of a mother who encouraged his criminal activities. And, of course, the Corcorans reminded her of Frank, who was the reason why she had sought distraction in Walter's stupid movie.

"If they'd made the film fifteen years earlier or fifteen years later, they would've just let you root for the villain, and then maybe killed him off at the end to show they were on the side of law and order. Like in *Public Enemy* from the thirties, or *Bonnie and Clyde* from the sixties. The fifties were all screwed up."

"Why don't you become a film critic, dear?" she said. "You know all about the subject, and I'm sure people would be interested in your observations."

He squirmed happily in his chair, smiling and making appreciative gestures. He was saved from giving a reply when the movie started again.

He wasn't playing with his gun. As far as she knew; it was in his desk, and there was a box of cartridges in the bottom drawer. He wouldn't stop her if she got up, walked to the desk, and loaded the gun. He might ask her what she was doing, but most of his attention would remain fixed on the television set. She would walk back across the room. Then, in one motion, she would put the muzzle to his head and pull the trigger. "Gee, hon, I'll miss the ending!" he might protest if he had time to guess what she was doing.

"What's the joke?" he asked, prepared to laugh with her.

She shook her head and nodded toward the television set, effectively diverting him.

The autopsy would disclose whiskey in his stomach. The television listings would reveal that he could have been watching one of the films that often inspired him to play with his gun.

"Don't they have a test they can give you to see if you fired a gun?" she had asked Frank once.

"It isn't conclusive. And if it detects anything, which it often doesn't, all it detects is nitrogen, so you can tell them you were fertilizing your lawn or mixing up a batch of laughing gas for your next wild party."

"Do they take laughing gas at wild parties?"

"You're pretty naïve for a would-be murderess."

That was when Frank had still thought of it as a game. She'd never thought of it entirely as a game, or so she'd told herself, but when he'd gotten serious about it, she'd been scared off.

No – not exactly scared off, disgusted, that was more like it, disgusted by Frank's whining and by his cowardly way of contemplating the murder seriously only when he thought he had no other options. He'd said it was against his principles to kill her husband; but when he was staring at prison and disgrace – the just consequences of his stupid and vicious acts – he abandoned his principles.

She kept trying to make allowances for him.

An excess of zeal, the heat of the chase, had made him try to frame Raymond so crudely. And during their last meeting he had been in a state of shock, half-drunk, and under severe pressure: few men could have acted well in such circumstances. Not all of them would have fallen apart like Frank, though.

Even when she tried to make allowances, she was faced with an unflattering picture of her lover. Despite his grandiose ambitions, he had plodded along during most of his adult life in a job that was probably only a little more demanding than Walter's. And he did his job like an enthusiastic kid, breaking the rules whenever he met frustration. The flashy clothes, the fire-engine red convertible, the two guns – these weren't the pardonable eccentricities of a serious adult; these were the realizations of an adolescent's daydreams. To Frank, they were important props for his unstable personality.

"This is all I've got left," he'd whined, caressing his hideous gun. And then, in effect, he'd threatened to hold his breath until he turned blue if she left him.

She could say one good thing for him: he hadn't called her since that day, begging her to reconsider, apologizing, or making new suicide threats. And even though she found it commendable that he hadn't called, it annoyed her.

She'd wanted to call him. Scarcely a waking moment

passed when she wasn't conscious of the telephone as a presence in the house, waiting for her to pick it up and call him. She knew what he was, but she wanted him. She wanted his easy laughter, his quick wit, but most of all she wanted his electrifying touch. Sometimes the desire for that touch was like a pain, and sometimes she had to relieve it by using Walter as a – what was that stupid word Frank had taught her? – as a dildo.

"What's so funny?" Walter asked, and she saw that a commercial was being shown.

"Nothing, dear. Maybe I've drunk too much." She got up and refilled her glass from the bottle by his chair. "It's just that I can't watch James Cagney without thinking of all those dumb Cagney imitations."

"'You're the dirty rat who shot my brother,'" Walter obligingly supplied.

"Exactly."

"Do you sometimes feel that we're in a rut?"

It took her a moment to realize that he wasn't echoing a line from some commercial on the tube, but that he had actually come up with that question on his own. She couldn't help laughing, and it was hard to stop. His comment had been like the caption of a cartoon, something one hamster on a wheel might ask another.

When she had managed to get herself under control, she asked: "In what way, Walter?"

"Well, you know, in all sorts of ways. You see the same friends all the time; you do the same things. I go to the office and do the same things; I come home and work on my railroad or watch a movie. We go to bed." He added with a sickening leer: "Only, that's been great, lately."

"If you're building up to the suggestion that we go and fuck, dear, just say the word," she said gloomily, staring into her glass.

"Oh. No. I wasn't, actually." Timidly, he said, "Do you want to?"

"I want whatever you want," she sighed.

"I'm glad to hear that. I think you understand what I'm saying. That's why you laughed, wasn't it, when I said we were in a rut? I mean, you understand. Here we are in the twentieth century, you know. God is dead, or maybe he's taking a long lunch."

"Where did you hear that one?"

"I didn't; I just thought of it. Anyway, here we are, completely free, but we're not, you know, fulfilling ourselves, doing what we want to, living out our fantasies."

"The movie is on, Walter."

"Oh, I've seen it," he said, shocking her into attentiveness. Whatever he wanted to say must be serious. "Anyway, the good part is the end, where he says, 'Made it, Ma! Top of the world!'"

"Is that the kind of fantasy you want to live out? Getting blown up on top of a gasoline storage tank?"

He laughed. "Yeah, when I go, that's how I'd like to do it. Only I don't want to go yet. There's things I want to do, things I've always imagined doing, but I'll never do them, because we're in a rut."

"What sort of things?"

"Well, I've read about these places in New York where people go and, you know, do all kinds of things."

"That sounds great. What is it, Grand Central Station? A supermarket? You have to be more specific."

"Well, what they do is, like they go swimming naked, or dancing, and they just make love with whoever they feel like doing it with."

"You aren't suggesting —" she had to stop to bring her laughter under control "— that we join a swingers' club, are you?"

"No, no, of course not!" he said with some heat. "What I mean is, they're living out their fantasies the way most people never do. The way we never do. What difference does it make; we're all going to die. But why die without doing the things you want to?"

"Grab all the gusto you can!" she cried with false enthusiasm, but her irony escaped him.

"That's what I mean!" he said brightly. "That's exactly what I'm trying to say! Have you ever made love to another girl?"

"What?" she cried when the unexpected question had sunk in. "What kind of a question is that? Of course not!"

"It's a question, that's all," he said mildly, with a shrug. "Can't we be honest with each other, and ask personal questions?"

She didn't want Walter to ask her personal questions, or any other kind: she wanted him to go back to his movie and leave her alone. But she said, "Sure."

"Have you ever had a fantasy about doing it?"

"Making love to another woman? Yes, I guess I have. I even did it, if you must know, but I was only thirteen."

"You did, huh? Hmm." His interest in her answer was oddly remote, like that of an anthropologist quizzing a savage. "Have you ever thought about making love to two men at once?"

She giggled, blamed the whiskey, and made an effort to bring herself under control. She said, "Yes."

"Have you ever done it?"

"*Walter!*" she cried. "Are you out of your mind?"

"Well, there you are," he said with the smug air of Perry Mason demolishing a witness. "You have this fantasy you've never lived out. Wouldn't you like to?"

"No, to be absolutely honest with you, I wouldn't," she said earnestly, trying to put a brake on his lunacy.

"There are all kinds of fantasies. Some of them are constructive, but some of them are inappropriate, and some of them are downright sick. The fantasy that I foolishly admitted to – it falls somewhere between the last two categories. It's not something I'm dying to try."

"You're just uptight, that's all," he said, still smug. "You wouldn't think about it unless you found it pleasant. And it stands to reason that doing it would be more pleasant than thinking about it."

She had a devastating rebuttal: to describe her favorite fantasy of blowing his brains out with his pistol. She was strongly tempted to tell him about it, but she fought the temptation.

"How about being in bed with a man and a woman?" he dropped into the strained silence. "Have you ever thought about that?"

"No, that isn't one of my fantasies," she said, and she got up to refill her glass. "Really, Walter, you're missing the good part. See? They're in the oil refinery."

"Never mind that," he said impatiently. "You see, that's my favorite fantasy."

"What is? Having sex with a man and a woman?"

Her misunderstanding had been deliberate, and she had the satisfaction of seeing him flustered. "No, of course not, hon, that isn't what I mean! What I mean is, making love to two women at once. I've always wanted to do that."

She thought of several amusing comments, but she bit them back. Walter was quite serious about his suggestion, and it appalled her; but, she was surprised to discover, not entirely. It would be *different,* anyway, and more of a distraction than watching TV.

"You want to do that?" she said.

Having presented his case, he seemed unable to face her; or maybe the movie had grabbed him. He nodded, watching the screen.

"Well, what the hell," she said.

"Made it, Ma! Top of the world!" James Cagney shouted tinnily into the silence that followed, and the gas tank erupted beneath him.

"That's great," Walter said. "Gee, hon, that's really swell! I never in a million years thought you'd say yes. It's really wonderful, being able to talk to you like this, being able to tell you what's really on my mind. It's like – I don't know, maybe this will sound like an insult, but I don't mean it that way, it's like you've grown up in the past couple of months."

Maybe he was right. She had matured, been turned into a woman by a real – no, not by a real – man, by just another adolescent, one whose fantasies ran more to violence than to the grubbier side of sex. She recalled the titillating sensation of superiority she'd felt with Sonny Corcoran, and she was struck by the irony of it; she was superior to all the men in her life. She wondered if that would always be the case.

"I guess I'm going to be one of the women in your fantasy, right, Walter? Do you have somebody else in mind, or do I have to provide her?"

His embarrassment was so acute that he feigned absorbing interest in a commercial for toupees. But maybe his interest was real. Maybe he planned to get one, in line with his new image as a swinger.

"You're laughing – but I mean, you mean it, don't you? What you said? You'll do it?"

"What, get another woman?" she laughed. She made a quick mental rundown of her acquaintances until she came to Suzy Deck –

Oh, Christ.

"No, that's not what I'm talking about," he said, not noticing what must have been her ghastly expression. "That's all set – or, what I mean is, there's this girl at the mill who's had her eye on me."

So she could see when your back was turned and say, "toot-toot," she thought, but that thought led her back to Suzy and her mood worsened. She got up and poured another drink. Her gaze seemed magnetized by the desk as she poured.

"Why did you give Ma Corcoran an alibi for the night Suzy was murdered?" she asked before she even knew that she was going to ask it.

"Jesus! Talk about Sam Spade. How come you pull questions like that out of left field all the time?" Walter asked with sudden and uncharacteristic anger. "How do you even know about that?"

"This is where ,Sam Spade would say, 'I'll ask the questions, buddy,'" she said airily.

"No, he wouldn't," Walter grumbled, but his anger seemed to have dissipated. "That would be a cop's line. But if you must know, that's what I said because it was true. We met at my office so we could go over some papers there. I hold the mortgage on her house, and there are some other notes and things."

She settled back in her chair. "Walter the landlord. I never quite saw you in that role. Do you wear a black cape and a top hat and a waxed mustache? Does she have a beautiful daughter that you have evil designs on? Is that who's going to bed with us?"

"No, no, no, of course not!" Walter said.

"What's she like?"

"Who?"

"Ma Corcoran."

Walter brooded for a moment, and then startled her by saying: "Circe."

A classical allusion was the last thing she'd expected from Walter, especially one that seemed so apposite to all she'd heard about Ma: Circe, the witch who'd changed men into swine. She would have loved to hear all about his affair with her, the one that had presumably produced Sonny – for all she knew, the one that was still going on, Walter was so full of surprises lately – but she sensed that this wasn't the time to ask.

"When are we going to do all this?" she asked.

"Huh?"

"Play games with your little-sweetie from the mill," Katy said. "And how long has that been going on?"

"Nothing's been going on," Walter mumbled, and he blushed. "She, well, she was talking, you know, we were sort of kidding each other around, and she just happened to mention how she likes to do it with married couples, you know, because it's more sensible, there isn't any jealousy or like that, or sneaking around."

It sounded plausible. Walter had made a pass at one of his employees, and she'd fobbed him off with a joke that he'd taken seriously. Or maybe she had been serious. There were a lot of weird people running around loose.

"Well, when?" she persisted.

"I could get her over this evening." He added: "If you want me to."

"What the hell," she said, again using the answer that seemed most appropriate to this situation. "Shall I stick a third TV dinner in the oven?"

"What you might try to do, is, you might try not to drink so much."

"Walter, I think I'll be able to get into the spirit of this thing if I get a little bit drunk, I really do."

"You are –" he started to say, but then he cut himself short and went to the telephone.

He spoke quietly and briefly. She didn't eavesdrop – she couldn't have, with the television between her and Walter – but it sounded as if he was simply confirming a date. *The sly old devil,* she thought.

"Is it all set?" she asked when he returned, and he nodded. She said, "What does she look like?"

"Buxom, I guess that's the word. Blond. Blue eyes. Pretty, but not the way you are. Sort of like a jolly milkmaid in one of those old paintings."

Katy groaned quietly. "Corrupting the morals of a millhand. Walter, you make me feel as if we're a couple of incredibly corrupt aristocrats who live in a castle and do wicked things to the peasants."

Walter laughed with pleasure. "Yeah. It's a fun feeling, isn't it?"

When the jolly milkmaid appeared at the door a couple of hours later and introduced herself as Gretchen Slovik, it was all Katy could do to keep from whooping with laughter. She couldn't seem to stop giggling, though; but since Gretchen was an inveterate giggler, Katy's lapse went unnoticed.

Gretchen had been constructed with a lavish hand. Walter's "buxom" was more just than Sonny's description of her as "fat." Her wrists and ankles were tiny, and her waist was waspish. Her breasts were enormous, her hips ample. Her incredible head of blond hair would have done credit to a country-and-western star, and Katy believed it was not a wig. Her movements were impressive, less like those of a milkmaid than a lioness, and Katy began to wonder if this might just not turn out to be enjoyable.

"This is crazy, isn't it?" Gretchen said with a giggle as she entered. "You got a great house. You got anything to drink?"

"Sure, we have plenty of that," she said, leading Gretchen to the bar. "Walter is . . . Walter? Walter! I guess he's hiding."

"That's okay. Let's you and me have a drink and like get to know each other, you know? Wally said you don't go in for this kind of stuff, he wasn't even sure you'd do it."

"Wally is hell on wheels, isn't he? Here, help yourself."

Gretchen exclaimed over the huge assortment of bottles and then made for the vodka, which she poured straight over ice. She took a lime from the icebox under the bar, peeled it with the expertise of a bartender, and 'dropped a twist into her drink. Then she downed half the glass and looked at Katy Without batting a false eyelash.

"You don't have to do nothing if you don't want to, of course. That's my motto. I'll even go, if that's what you want."

"No, no, stay. I want to. I'm nervous, that's all."

Gretchen touched her arm with a lingering caress. Katy giggled as she remembered Sonny's description of her odor. All she could detect was an unexpectedly virginal whiff of Shalimar.

"Don't be nervous. It's the most natural thing in the world, isn't it? It's just playing, like in a game, like kids."

That seemed terribly philosophical for someone like Gretchen, and it eased some of her nervousness. She wondered where Walter had gotten to. Maybe he really was hiding, scared by the imminent realization of his fantasy. Or maybe he was doing obscure Oriental exercises to prepare himself.

"Walter says you've done this before," Katy said.

"Wally is silly," Gretchen said unexceptionably, and she giggled. "I do whatever I feel like. What say we take our clothes off and give him a shock when he comes in?"

That struck Katy as a marvelously funny idea, and she raced Gretchen to implement it. The thought of Walter, stodgy old Walter, coming into his familiar bar in his familiar home to find two naked women sipping drinks was irresistible. She couldn't wait to see the look on his face.

Only ,when they were sitting naked on the bar stools did she recall that stodgy old Walter had thought the whole thing up in the first place.

"He has hidden depths," Katy said. "I always thought of him as a – a lump."

Gretchen crossed her legs, which were sleek and firm. She'd kept on her high-heeled black pumps, like a model in a masturbator's magazine. Her breasts were real, and unexpectedly well suspended for their size. It was Katy's turn to giggle as she remembered her admission of lesbian fantasies. It might be said that Walter, of all people, was making one of her dreams come true.

Walter appeared unexpectedly from the stairs to the second floor. He seemed oddly preoccupied, even worried, but that expression soon gave way to a rewarding one of pure shock. Then he leered like a dirty-minded schoolboy as he came forward.

"Hi, Gretchen. Gee, hon, I've never seen the bar looking so good. It's like –"

"Like a fancy whorehouse in a movie," Katy supplied, and Gretchen laughed so hard that she spilled her drink.

He kissed Katy and caressed her bare breast as she threw herself into her response. Then he kissed Gretchen, and she felt a twinge that she couldn't quite identify. Gretchen tickled the obvious bulge at his crotch and tried to unzip his fly, but he stepped back. Not to be undone, Katy leaned forward and kissed Gretchen, who opened her mouth and tickled her tongue with hers. Walter coughed politely.

"Shall we go upstairs?" he said.

"I got to refresh my drink first," Gretchen said, slipping off her stool and going behind the bar. She poured a tumbler of vodka and added a single ice cube as an afterthought.

"Refresh mine like that, while you're at it," Katy said. "I think I've been drinking bourbon or something. Why don't you take your pants off, Walter? You've overdressed."

"Let's go upstairs," he said.

"Not until you take your pants off," Katy said.

She turned to accept her suicidal drink from Gretchen while Walter complied. She winked at Gretchen, who winked back. She saw that Walter was naked and his penis was fully erect. She usually had to tease him a little bit first. He was making an obvious but successful effort to hold in his belly.

"Why don't we do it on the floor?" Katy suggested, and then she sang a few bars of the Beatles' song, "Why Don't We Do It in the Road?"

"Come on, it's more fun in a bed," Gretchen urged, and Walter eagerly seconded her.

Once they were upstairs, she had to admit they'd been right. The big bed, covered in warm reds and browns, looked inviting. Walter must have been up here turning on all the lights in the large room. Even the lights at her dressing table were on. She supposed he wouldn't even take his bridge out for this event.

"Walter usually turns the lights out," Katy said.

"Looking is half the fun," Gretchen said, and she leaned forward to touch Katy's nipple with her skillful tongue.

Katy had no idea how to begin in such a situation, but they took the initiative away as they both worked to arouse her. Walter kissed her right breast, Gretchen her left. She lay back on the bed. Walter moved down to lick her sex while Gretchen kissed her passionately on the lips. Katy returned the kiss with equal passion and began to twist her hips under Walter's surprisingly exciting touches. She stroked Gretchen between the legs and found that she was lubricating copiously.

"I want to kiss you there," she whispered in Gretchen's ear.

"Do Wally first," Gretchen answered sensibly, also in a soft whisper. "It's his party."

She slithered around and put Walter's penis in her mouth. For the first time, she found that she was enjoying it. She was having a wonderful time, and she knew that couldn't be entirely attributed to the liquor. Who needed Frank? She realized with a little thrill that it was the first time in a long time that she'd thought of him. She sucked enthusiastically.

Gretchen nudged her aside and began to suck Walter's penis. She slipped her head between Gretchen's legs and tongued her vulva gently. Sonny was crazy. It was a sensual experience akin to eating oysters. The slight, tart tang of the sea was there, the slippery texture.

Walter's tongue became suddenly more deft, more exciting. She realized that it was Gretchen's tongue. The glimmering edge of something wonderful began to impinge on her awareness: While Katy lay beneath her, Walter entered Gretchen. Seen from this unimagined angle it was rather impressive, like a dirigible entering a hanger. She leaned back to touch Walter's scrotum with her tongue.

About to break free of her body's cage and fly, Katy was dashed back to reality by an inexplicable crash. She twisted out from under Gretchen. She stared at the wall of white cabinets opposite the bed. One of the doors hung halfway open. She sensed rather than saw movement inside.

"What the *hell!*" she yelled.

"Katy . . ." Walter said, but he was too involved in fucking Gretchen to protest. Gretchen's efforts to detain her were ineffective.

Katy hurled herself off the bed and flung open the

door of the cabinet. She needed no formal introduction to know that the naked woman who crouched in the closet, the woman with the frizzy red hair and the glassy eyes who was stroking herself to an orgasm, the woman who had been watching them all this time, was Ma Corcoran.

Katy began to scream and throw things.

Chapter Thirteen

Now that Katy had unexpectedly agreed to execute the plan, Frank began to have serious second thoughts. It had been easy to strike melodramatic poses and talk seriously of murder when he'd been drunk, when he still hadn't gotten over the destruction of his case against the Corcorans and the loss of his job; now, cold sober and trying to make some reasonable plan for the future, it wasn't so easy. It struck him that it would be more sensible than murdering Walter to ask him for a job as night watchman at the mill.

The killing itself didn't bother him too much, even though he'd never killed a man in cold blood before. He knew he could do it. Just squeeze the trigger, that's all there was to it.

Only later would the difficulties arise, and they would be serious difficulties.

As he'd told Katy, she would be the prime suspect under any circumstances: should Walter happen to slip and crack his skull on the bathtub tonight, entirely on his own, she would be questioned, her private life would be subjected to scrutiny. What happened after that would depend largely on the instinct of the investigating officer. LaPlante, who would probably be that officer, might be slow, but he was no fool. The slightest suggestion that there was another man in her life would make him dig deeper. And if he knew that man was Frank, he wouldn't stop digging until he came up with something.

They had undoubtedly made a few slips. There probably were people who could testify to having seen them together. He could explain that by pointing out that he was working on the Maniac investigation at the time, questioning her about her encounter with Sonny Corcoran or – her friendship with Suzy Decker. Now that he was no longer on the force, he could give no such explanation. They couldn't afford to be seen together anymore.

The backyards of the big houses on High Street ended at a deep ravine which ran all the way down to Railroad Avenue on the sleazier side of town. Near the railroad bridge, where it widened and ended, it was an unofficial dump; as it grew steeper and narrower on its way to the high-rent district, it became thickly wooded. At Katy's suggestion, Frank took this route on his way to her house. He didn't want to be observed knocking on her front door while Walter was at work, nor could he run the risk of parking his conspicuous car in her neighborhood.

Despite these precautions, he still believed that he hadn't made up his mind to kill Walter. He wanted to see Katy, that was all, he had to see her. He hadn't even so much as heard her voice in a week; and the sound of it on the telephone this morning had made him tremble. He was just being careful, and leaving his options open.

Katy – he loved her, he wanted her all to himself, but she was also the principal difficulty in the murder plot. By killing Walter, he would become tied to her for the rest of his life in the bond of a shared secret that would be far more obligating than any marriage. The bond might become intolerable to either of them; and the woman bound to him would have already demonstrated her willingness to kill for what she wanted. These considerations, much more than the murder itself, scared him.

He began to sweat as he walked up the path, and he knew that it wasn't just because of the heat of the day. He took off his jacket and paused for a moment to listen, but all he heard were birds and the gurgle of the brook that had carved the ravine. Kids came here to play, and an occasional birder or dog-walker might be encountered on a summer afternoon, but so far he had seen and heard no one. He started again up the path.

He thought about Katy's obvious agitation this morning. His phone had rung. He'd picked it up.

"Frank," she'd said, with no other greeting, "we're going to snuff the son-of-a-bitch."

"Wait –"

"We're leaving for the lake this afternoon. Come here at two and pick up the gun. Come on foot, by way of the ravine. A flight of stone steps leads up to our yard, it's the only one, you can't miss it, and I'll leave the gate at the top unlocked."

"Wait a minute. Why this sudden change of heart?"

"I love you, that's why," she'd said, hanging up.

She hadn't sounded like it, except, possibly, in those last words, when she'd deliberately softened her voice. He was more inclined to believe that Walter had done something outrageous. If you love someone, you don't let him dangle for a week and then call him up to speak briskly of murder. She could be, as he'd had occasion to observe before, a tough customer.

But he was grateful for the chance to see her. It was more than he'd expected. The last time they'd met, he knew, he'd succeeded in making a complete asshole of himself. But however he'd behaved, Walter had apparently managed to outdo him, and she'd made her choice. Perhaps they could arrange something less than murder: like going away together, fleeing his legal troubles and her insufferable husband, arranging to take a large chunk of Walter's assets when they left.

He had reached the foot of the steps, carved into the rock face of the ravine. Around the time of the Civil War, when the Burroughs mansion had been the only house on High Street, the ravine must have been part of the garden. Even without a knowledge of botany, he could see that the trees and shrubs around him were cultivated plants that had run wild, unlike the second-growth foliage of the lower ravine.

He sighed. He could spend only so much time admiring the greenery. He turned and reluctantly started up the steps.

He paused, distracted by a noise behind him. It would be one of those birders or dog-walkers. Frank hurried up the steps, glancing from time to time over his shoulder, but he saw no one and assumed he hadn't been seen.

"Now," he said to Katy as she opened the back door to him, "what –"

She silenced him with a kiss. It was a very convincing kiss, but he still felt that he had to ask the question: "What made you change your mind?"

"I told you, Frank, I love you," she said, and it was hard to doubt her when he was looking down into her big, dark eyes. "I didn't know how much until this week. I did a lot of thinking, and I've decided you're right. It's your last big chance. It's mine, too. We have to take it."

"What's Walter done?"

His guess had been right. His question jolted her.

But she recovered quickly. "He's been himself," she said. "That's more than enough reason to . . . do it."

"Killing him over a domestic spat isn't very sensible. You might cool off and regret it after he's dead. You might start feeling guilty. LaPlante can be very fatherly and understanding. He'll encourage you to cry on his shoulder and tell him all about it."

"I can't see myself crying on somebody's shoulder, Frank," she said coldly. "How about you?"

She was convincing enough to be a little scary. He had no doubts about his own ability to carry it through. He found that he had to clear his throat before he could say, "All right. We'll do it."

She led him to Walter's study, a room bigger than his own apartment. She went to the mantel and took the keys to the desk from an ornate little chest. He looked around the room and felt a curious sensation. The fireplace, the leather chairs, the books, the pictures, even the room itself, now unfamiliar, would be his before long. This would be home. Maybe not. Maybe the scandal surrounding the trial – he felt almost certain there would be a trial – would be so great that they'd have to go live in a villa in the south of France. He wouldn't object.

"What's so funny?"

"The famous TV set," he lied. "Is this where he does his target practice?"

She nodded abstractedly, fumbling with the keys as she bent over the desk. That slim, fine body, the long hair shading her lovely face – that would be his, too, for keeps. He wondered if burglars felt this exhilaration when they pierced the defenses of a wealthy home.

"Suppose he decides to take his gun with him to the lake?" he said.

She glanced at him with irritation. "He never has before."

"Maybe somebody knows that, and will point it out."

"Everybody knows that he's afraid of blacks and kids and anarchists and his own workers. And the Full Moon Maniac is still running loose. It won't need explaining."

"You've convinced me. He'll probably take it. The only sensible thing is to wait until the last minute, just before you leave the house. If he doesn't take it, you do."

She found the pistol and the cartridges and banged them down on top of the desk. She shoved in the drawers and locked them with a flourish.

"Absolutely not. I am not going to open the door to you at the lake, put the gun in your hand, and point you toward my husband. All right, I'm being irrational, you don't have to tell me, but that's a scene I am not going to play. Take the gun now. That's how we'll do it."

"You're so masterful," he sighed with heavy sarcasm; but he picked up the gun. "Son-of-a-bitch is loaded and ready to go. Maybe his Humphrey Bogart impression was more vivid than you thought." He pushed out the cylinder and caught light from the window inside the barrel. "Didn't anybody ever tell him you're supposed to clean these things?"

She ignored him as she took a paper from the pocket of her jeans and spread it on the desk. He saw that it was a detailed map of the house by the lake and its surroundings.

"This is the road you'll use, a gravel road. It comes out of the main highway two miles away, at Hobson's Corners. This is a wooden bridge. There's a path leading under it that a car can follow. Leave your car under the bridge. A hundred yards beyond it, you pick up the path to our house. It starts at a gate in a broken-down wooden fence. You go straight across an overgrown meadow that slopes up to a wood. You'll be able to see the lights of our house from the top of the slope; and I'll make sure that plenty of them are on. You –"

"Is the electricity turned on?" he interrupted.

"I called them yesterday, and they assured me it would be."

"Even before you called me," he observed.

"The path to the house is downhill, but it's not especially steep," she said, ignoring the observation. "If you take your time, you should have no trouble following it. But try to memorize its course as well as you can, because you won't want to waste any time when you leave the house. Don't use a flashlight, whatever you do. Somebody might see it from the other side of the lake."

"I'm not the Last of the Mohicans, you know. I grew up in town. I wasn't even a Boy Scout."

"It's *easy*, believe me! The trees are all cedars, with no undergrowth beneath them. Even if you wander off the path you won't trip over anything. You'll be able to see the lights of the house all the time.

"Now," she said, "you should allow forty-five minutes for the walk from the bridge, that gives you a safety margin of twenty minutes. Arrive at the back door – the side away from the lake – at nine-thirty. Just walk in." She spread out a second sheet, a diagram of the house, on top of the first. "Don't enter by the kitchen door, use the one on the left. It opens on a hall that passes the kitchen, the butler's pantry, the dining room, the main stairs, and then leads into the living room. That's where we'll be."

"Where will the butler be?"

She laughed for the first time. "We don't have one, that's just what the damned thing is called."

"And how can you be sure Walter will be in the living

room at nine-thirty? Suppose he's out taking a stroll?"

"I checked the television listings. *The Big Sleep* is on, it starts at nine o'clock, and he wouldn't miss that one for a thousand dollars in cash. I'll start him drinking when he gets home, here. I'll open a bottle of wine with dinner. I'll keep his glass filled while he's watching the movie."

"And when I come charging down the hall, he'll be in the bathroom taking a piss. Next thing I know, he'll be in back of me with his shotgun."

"First, you don't come charging down the hall. You come in like Sandburg's fog, on little cat feet. I've noticed that's one of your talents. If Walter should leave the room for any reason, I'll keep a conversation going with him. I'll ask him questions about the movie that require detailed answers – it's a good one for that, incidentally, and he's the only person I know who pretends to understand the plot. If Walter has left the living room, you'll hear him jabber ring about the movie, and you'll know just where he is. Wait for him to return to the living room. He'll be sitting in a wing chair with his back to you." With no more emotion than she'd shown in presenting the other details of her plan, she concluded: "Come up from behind and shoot him in the right side of the head."

"What then?"

"Get out fast. I'll be speeding around the lake to wake up the people at the general store so I can use the phone."

"You mean, we, aren't going to raise a couple of glasses over his body and say, 'To crime!'?"

"No, we aren't. I'm going to be a hysterical widow, and believe me, it isn't going to be an act. That'll be the best part of it. So don't even speak to me; it might have a calming effect. If nothing happens, we'll arrange to meet a couple of months after the funeral, but don't call me, don't even think about me, until then."

"I'll need money for a lawyer. For that Sonny business."

"Get a job," she said shortly.

"God damn it," he breathed.

"Frank, it was you who explained all this to me in the first place. A big, fat check of mine, made out to you – even a substantial withdrawal of cash from my account – isn't that exactly what they'll be looking for?"

She was right, of course, but he was desperate for some assurance that he wasn't going to pull the trigger and drop out of her life. It hadn't occurred to him until now, but once he'd shot Walter, she could pick up all the marbles and walk away. His threats would be empty: he could expose her only by exposing himself, and his would be the greater guilt before the law.

Instead of saying what was on his mind, he said, "Did you leave any preliminary sketches for these maps lying around the house?"

"Of course not," she said, and she forestalled his attempt to pick them up. "And these aren't leaving the room." She carried the maps to a coffee table, where she picked up a heavy silver lighter. She flicked it on and began to burn the only physical evidence that he could have held against her.

"You have a lot of confidence in my memory," he said.

"You're no dope," she said, and he supposed he could take that more than one way. "Have we covered everything?"

"Not everything," he said, moving toward her.

She stood by the fireplace, concentrating on the job of destroying the last corner of the paper without burning her fingers. "What?" she said without looking up.

He grabbed her around the waist and half-carried her to Walter's desk, where he swept the clutter to the floor with his free arm. He dumped her on the desk and forced her to lie back. When she tried to push him away, he seized both her slender wrists in one hand and held her down.

"What are you doing? What the *hell* do you think you're doing?"

"Taking your pants off," he said, and he did it ungently. "Literally and figuratively."

"You bastard! You prick! Let me go!" She bit his hand, drawing blood, but he squeezed her wrists until she screamed.

He dropped his trousers to his ankles. He wasn't at all hard, and he was amused by the thought of how foolish he would look if, after this beginning, he proved impotent. He stared at the curly wedge between her thighs and remembered the exquisite, unique softness of that hair as he pumped himself with his hand. He twisted to catch her vicious kick on his hip.

Speaking from the side of his mouth in the gravelly voice of a tough guy from some *film noir,* he snarled: "You better come across; baby, or I won't put the chill on your old man."

She shrieked again, but this time with laughter. "You idiot! I can't do it!"

"That makes two of us," he said. "Oops, correction: one of us."

He slid between her flailing legs and guided himself to his goal. It was as tight and dry as a landlord's lips, but he shoved. Her hands free, she hit him on the ear and made it ring. He dug his fingers into her buttocks and lifted her to met his thrust.

Two or three painful and uncertain minutes passed before she began to respond. "I hate your fucking guts, you bastard," she moaned, but her tone belied her words.

Once he had gained her cooperation, he concentrated solely on her pleasure. His attitude, often cold and detached during sex, was icy. The satisfaction he derived from her kisses and moans and grunts and twists and shudders was intellectual satisfaction. He felt that this was one of the most important things he had ever done, that it wouldn't be too much to say that his life depended on his success; and he succeeded.

"I'm sore," she grumbled when she next spoke.

"I'm sore, too, and I've probably got – blood poisoning," he said, sucking at the wound on his hand. "Being a rapist isn't as easy as it's cut out to be."

"Filthy Frank," she said.

He stared at her, puzzled. "Why do they call me that?"

"Like in *Dirty Harry*, shithead."

He roared with laughter. "Oh, Christ! That's wonderful! I thought it was an insult." He stopped laughing. "Only now there's no point in them ever calling me that again."

"Yes, they will. It will be all over the front page of every paper in the country when they catch you for putting the chill on my old man."

"They won't catch us."

"No. We're not just sexy, we're smart. I'll always call you Filthy Frank, if you like it."

"Thanks. But if you're so smart, you take the gun. You don't have to hand it to me. Leave it on the kitchen sink."

"Yeah, with a note: 'Dear Frank, this is the end the bullets come out of, stick it in hubby's ear.' It is smart, Frank. What if Walter decides to take his gun, and decides to have a shoot-out with Humphrey Bogart while he's watching *The Big Sleep*? You'd have to come into the room and take the gun away from him. You might bruise him in the struggle – or he might even shoot you. Trust me. I'll tell him a story that will convince him. I have one in mind."

Her argument was persuasive, as all her arguments were, but he knew that her real reason was emotional. He decided to go along with her. It seemed like the one irrational point in their scheme, but he didn't see how it could undo them, if everything she said was true. He took his leave with Walter's belly-buster in the left-hand pocket of his jacket.

He walked down the ravine with a springy step, less aware of his surroundings than he might have been. He had just made love to Katy for the first time in a week: a much better way to think of it than for the last time in more than two months. But when their enforced separation was over, he knew, she would want him again.

Halfway down the ravine, Sonny Corcoran hit him between the shoulders with a baseball bat.

Some instinct told him it was Sonny even before he hit the ground. He didn't know it was a baseball bat until, rolling over, he saw it raised over his head.

"You dirty cocksucker!" Frank screamed in agony as he just managed to roll away from the blow that would have squashed his head like a melon.

"You're dead, Filthy Frank. You're a fucking dead man," Sonny grunted, scrambling after him with the bat raised.

Frank feinted another roll away from Sonny, then made a lunge for his knees. He gripped them as his last hold on life. With more intelligence than Frank would have believed him capable of, Sonny refrained from overhand swings; he plunged the bat down vertically, like a pile-driver, aiming for Frank's head. He missed, striking Frank's shoulders with numbing blows. Frank thrust his head between Sonny's legs.

Using more strength than he thought he had, he heaved himself erect, lifting Sonny off the ground and throwing him over his back.

Gritting his teeth against the pain, Frank turned to face Sonny as he rose. He reached for the .357 Magnum under his left armpit. His right hand, sore and swollen from Katy's bite, couldn't fit itself immediately around the butt. A sidearm swing of the bat connected with his elbow, immobilizing his right arm.

"I'll teach you to fuck with me and Ma, you fucking pig!" Sonny roared, drawing the bat back over his shoulder for the final blow.

Frank pulled the .38 from his left-hand pocket and shot Sonny just below the beltbuckle. Sonny staggered backward with the impact, turning. The bat fell from his hand. The big, raw splotch on the back of his T-shirt told Frank that Walter had loaded his piece with soft-nose bullets.

"Kill your ass, you fucker," Sonny gasped, reaching for the bat with one hand as he clutched the wound in his belly with the other. "You ain't – I mean, *haven't* even –"

Frank knew that Sonny's wound was mortal. Staggering, white-faced, already going into deep shock, he posed no threat: except that it would take him a long time to die, and he might talk. As Sonny swung the bat, missed, and collapsed on his hands and knees, Frank extended the gun at arm's length and shot him behind the right ear. Sonny's dark glasses flew off. His face, punched out by the hydrostatic shock of his exploding brain, became a lumpy mask.

"And the same goes for your Ma," Frank growled, jamming the pistol back into his pocket.

He staggered down the ravine, listening hard. Soon he heard people calling, above and behind him. He had played in the ravine as a kid. He knew that the only exit lay at the end. He forced himself into a stumbling run. When the call came in, a smart dispatcher might send a car to the end of the ravine. Somebody screamed behind him. Sonny's body must be visible from the rim. The call would go in soon, if it hadn't already. If he met a birder or a dog-walker on the way out, he would shoot him dead. What about a kid? He didn't know. He drew the Magnum clumsily with his left hand.

It had been self-defense, more or less, his own broken bones proved it: but self-defense against the star witness in the state versus Frank Buchanan? Nobody would buy it. They'd throw him under a jail for the rest of his life. The state would argue that he'd lured Sonny here to kill him; that Sonny had prudently brought a baseball bat and fought for his life.

The execution of Katy's perfect crime was the least of his worries, but that had gone down the drain, too. When two citizens of a city the size of Armitage are shot on the same day with the same caliber bullet, somebody is bound to make a ballistics comparison. Soft-nose bullets are not ideal for such comparisons, but they can be made. The first round, which had gone right through Sonny, probably hadn't struck any big bones. When they found it, they could use it for textbook illustrations.

If only Walter had been downstairs playing with his trains! He shot Sonny – his illegitimate son, who was pressuring him for one reason or another – in back of his house, then shot himself out of remorse. But Walter, according to Katy, was at the mill now, with a couple of thousand witnesses to back up his story.

And there was another good reason for calling off the plot. He had, he believed, a broken arm and a dislocated shoulder. He would be lucky to get to the end of the ravine. Driving to the lake was out of the question.

He drove himself harder as he heard a whooping siren in the distance: ahead of him, the clever bastards! His terror was not unmixed with a certain pride in the department.

But the ravine had widened. He could see the railroad bridge. He staggered through piles of junk and debris. The siren was alarmingly close. He crawled into the back of a rusted old car and stared at the blue sky through the glassless window, sobbing for breath. Feet pounded past him.

Hey, guys! he wanted to shout. *I just snuffed the Full Moon Maniac!*

He wanted to laugh, but he couldn't quite do it.

Chapter Fourteen

Katy had just stunned Walter – whom she'd barely spoken to since the night of the fiasco in the bedroom – by pouring him a drink and pleasantly asking him how his day had been when the front doorbell rang. It was the police.

"Hello, Mrs. Burroughs," said the uniformed policeman, whom she didn't know. "Sorry to bother you, but we're checking for people who might have heard the shots this afternoon, or seen anything out of the ordinary."

"Who is it, hon?" Walter called, drifting up behind her.

"Shots? I didn't – oh, about an hour ago. I thought it was boys with, firecrackers. I didn't –" her heart stopped beating "– Who was shot?"

"Shot?" Walter echoed. "Who?"

"Kid named Sonny Corcoran, down in the ravine in back of your house."

Katy was shaken, but she had the presence of mind to look for Walter's reaction. It was unnerving. His face turned gray, his whole body sagged, he seemed to age ten years before her eyes. Unexpected sympathy almost moved her to take his arm.

The second cop, who hadn't spoken before, took in the scene and said, "Don't let it throw you. He was a rotten punk."

"He was a human being!" Walter said angrily.

"If you say so," the second cop said in a bored tone.

"Did you see anything?" the first cop asked.

"I was at work," Walter said, turning and walking away down the hall.

"No, I didn't," Katy said. "As I said, I didn't think anything of it at the time. Kids are always setting off firecrackers down there."

"Yeah, I know," the first cop said glumly. "That's what everybody says."

She felt she ought to ask: "Was it a robbery, or –"

"Sonny tried to clobber somebody with his baseball bat, that was his hobby, and he picked the wrong guy," the second cop interrupted. "It's nothing for you to worry about."

They left, and Katy was just beginning to weigh the startling news, when Walter shouted from his study: "Where the hell is my gun? What did you do with my gun?"

She walked quickly to the study, composing himself on the way. "I didn't do anything with your gun, Walter," she said. "Where did you leave it?"

"In my desk, of course! Locked."

"What do you want to do, dear, shoot Bugs Bunny? There's nothing else on TV at this hour."

She took a jerky, involuntary step backward as he advanced on her. She had never thought him capable of violence until this minute.

"I don't want your goddamned wise-ass bitchy answers, do you hear me? I want to know what you did with my gun."

He stopped a few paces off and stared at her, his fists

clenched, his body trembling.

"And I told you, I didn't do anything with your silly gun." She was surprised at how calm her voice sounded. "Why on earth do you want it?"

"Why?" he echoed. Some of the steam leaked out of him as he gestured despairingly and turned away. "Somebody got shot almost in our own backyard. Under the circumstances, don't you think I ought to check and see if my gun is where it's supposed to be? And it isn't, is it? I think I should call the police."

She had envisioned that, as the most extreme line he might take. She was shaken by it, but she hit him with the salvo she had prepared: "Walter, when you invite people like Marjorie Corcoran and Gretchen Slovik into your home, you have to expect to find things missing. Have you checked the silverware?"

She breathed easier as she saw her words strike home. All the fight went out of him. She hadn't mentioned those names since Walter, in a blind panic, had bundled them half-naked out of the house while she shrieked and threw anything that came to hand after them.

"They wouldn't . . . I don't know," he mumbled.

"When the police come to investigate your missing gun, we'll have to tell them all about that. They'll want to know if any strangers have been in the house lately."

"I guess you're right. But look at this. Somebody's been fucking with my desk," he said, gesturing at the clutter she thought she'd recreated so skillfully.

On your desk, dear, she wanted to say, and she found it hard not to laugh. But she decided to press the offensive mercilessly. She said, "Maybe Sonny was here looking for his birth certificate."

Harpooning Walter was so easy that it was almost no fun. He let out a strangled cry of shock and pain and looked away.

"You know about that," he stated.

"I told you about the night he approached me on the street. Basically, that's what he wanted to tell me. I didn't know you had it in you, Walter." She added bitterly, confronting a thought she had been repressing for a long time. "And all these years, I thought it was your fault that we didn't have any children."

"I don't know if it's true." He still refused to face her, and she realized with surprise that he was sobbing. "He thought so, and maybe . . . I don't know. He thought so because I had business with Ma – with Marjorie. You don't understand. I loved you then, I loved you with all my heart, but Marjorie . . . She was older. She knew things, everything. She could bring all my fantasies to life."

"Oh, come off it, Walter! I saw your dream girl."

"Looks have nothing to do with it. And she used to look better; she was even beautiful. First she let me do things, and then she made me do things, and the things kept getting worse. Her daughters – they were very young. Very young, I mean, children. She took Polaroid pictures; I didn't think anything of it at the time, it was like, you know, part of the fun, seeing ourselves. But she kept the pictures."

"Fun," she echoed dully.

"I told you, she made me do things!" he sobbed.

"Like give her money."

He hesitated. "Yes."

"And give her an alibi for Suzy's murder."

Again he hesitated. "Yes."

"And she was the one who wanted to see me make a fool of myself with you and that fat whore. Wasn't that her idea? Make Walter degrade his wife for her amusement?"

"Yes, yes, yes! And she made sure you found out, the bitch! Oh, the bitch!" He slammed his fists convulsively and repeatedly down on the desk. "I could kill her!"

"Why on earth did you let her do it? Why didn't you tell me about her? You're the one who's always saying we should talk more. Why didn't you talk about that, for God's sake! I could have helped you get out of her clutches."

She hadn't suspected that Walter could strike back, and when he did, it hit her like a physical blow: "She told me about you and that detective. Sonny used to follow you."

She couldn't think of a single thing to say.

"So, what was the difference?" he said, dry-eyed now, his voice cold. "You were just another whore like Gretchen. What difference did it make if you put on a show for Marjorie?"

"You contemptible creep!" she spat. "I knew you were dull and stupid and ignorant, I knew that your touch was repulsive to me, but I never realized what a truly slimy thing you are."

"Where's my gun?"

"I don't *know* where your goddamned gun is! Call the police, why don't you? Tell them that your bastard son by the woman who's been blackmailing you was shot this afternoon in your backyard and, by some strange coincidence, your gun is missing. You want me to call them?"

She walked briskly to his desk and picked up the receiver, but he reached out and depressed the hook.

"That detective . . ."

Good God, did he suspect? He couldn't! She asked sharply: "What about him?"

"Do you love him?"

She breathed again. He hadn't been thinking of Frank in relation to the gun; he'd just been indulging in a typical non sequitur. "Of course not. He fucks good. That's what all us whores like, didn't Gretchen ever tell you?"

Walter stood up. Colors exploded in her head, then each color changed to a different shade of pain. She gaped at him like a woman savaged by a rabbit as she touched her burning cheek. Before she could speak, he dropped to his knees and hugged her legs, sobbing against her thighs.

"I'm sorry. Oh, God, I'm sorry, I'm sorry, I'm sorry! I love you, Katy, I love you! I'll kill myself, I'll take a knife and cut off the hand that struck you, I will, I'll do it! Tell me to do it!"

"Calm down, Walter. Please. It's all right," she said. She was frightened and repelled by the excessiveness of his remorse. She sensed that it could easily swing back to rage.

"Don't leave me. Say you won't leave me. You can have him, you can have any man you want, as many as you want, just don't leave me alone."

"I won't leave you, Walter. I'll stay with you as long as you live," she said, dispassionately stroking the thinning hair on the skull that held such filthy secrets.

"Thank you," he sobbed, looking up at her. "You don't love him, do you?"

"No."

"It's just that he fucks good. That's all, isn't it?"

"Yes, Walter, that's all."

"I understand. I don't mind. I can still fuck you, can't I? If I let you have him?"

"Of course, Walter."

No man had ever disgusted her so much as Walter did at this minute. She had never imagined that any man, not even Walter, could disgust her so much. But these feelings were nothing compared to the disgust, the loathing, the complete physical revulsion that his next question provoked: "Could I watch sometime?"

She tried hard not to understand what he'd said. "Watch what?"

"You and him, you know. In bed."

"Walter, that's . . . sick," she said.

He bowed his head to kiss her sandaled feet. "I know, I'm disgusting, I'm not worthy of you, but I think that would be exciting, it would be so – humiliating. Marjorie always understood me; she always treated me worse than dirt. But I love you, Katy: You don't love me, of course you don't, nobody could. If you knew me, if you really knew me, you'd crush me under your foot like a worm."

I know you well enough for that, thanks. Aloud, she said, "Get up, Walter. Please. You're slobbering all over my shoes. We can talk when we get to the lake. I guess we have a lot to talk about now, don't we?"

He got up slowly, wearily, avoiding her eye. He drifted back toward the desk, staring at it in puzzlement.

"Has he ever been here, in this room? The detective?"

"No, dear, never. I always thought it would be like defiling our home to have a strange man here. I never imagined you'd get a kick out of it."

He ignored the thrust and went to the chest on the mantel. "The spare keys are still here," he said.

"Anyway, he's not a detective anymore. They fired him."

"I know. But if he solved some big crime on his own, they'd take him back, wouldn't they?"

"He's not interested in solving crimes anymore. He's fed up with the whole thing," she said.

"That's what he told you," he said enigmatically. "Sonny – maybe he was here. He's – he was sneaky. Marjorie could have sent him. But she didn't know where I kept my gun, or where I kept the keys to the desk." He turned and stared hard at her.

"Where do people keep guns, Walter? Not in the bathroom or the kitchen. The first place I'd look would be a bedside table. Then I'd look in a man's study, or den. In the desk. And if I were looking for keys, I'd look under the edge of the carpet. Then I'd look in a vase, or a box, like that chest sitting there in the middle of the mantel."

"I guess that makes sense," he said. "You're right. You didn't take it, did you?"

"Cut it out, Walter!" she shouted, and he winced. "Are we going to the lake, or aren't we? I'd like to get in a swim before dark."

"Okay, hon, sure, I guess so. What did I do with my drink? I need it, now."

"I'll get you a fresh one."

When he went upstairs to fetch the suitcases, Katy was sorely tempted to pick up the phone and ask Frank what had happened in the ravine. But she could think of no way in which Sonny's death could affect their plan; unless, of course, Frank had shot him with Walter's gun, but Frank was too smart for that.

She had thought about calling off the whole thing when she'd learned that Ma Corcoran knew about her and Frank. But she'd decided to go ahead. Ma's knowledge couldn't affect the plan either. She might try to blackmail them later, suspecting what they'd done, but she had no leverage. All she knew was what Sonny had told her, and Sonny was dead.

Walter said little all the way to the lake, but that wasn't unusual: driving required his utmost concentration and, even so, he was a terrible driver. She spent the time preparing her mind for what would come . . . It was surprisingly easy. Glancing sidelong at her wretch of a husband, she found herself looking forward to it eagerly. Her only regret was that she hadn't guessed that he was a sexual masochist. It would have made life more bearable, it might even have been enjoyable, to kick him and beat him and make love to other men in front of his eyes. If anyone deserved it, Walter did.

She thought of him and Ma Corcoran's little girls. She wondered what had become of them. Perhaps they had rebelled against their upbringing by entering a convent.

At the lake Katy took a nude swim with the thought of giving Walter a last thrill, but he didn't even bother to watch. He pottered about in the lodge, as he always called it. His father had used it as a hunting lodge, and it was still decorated with antlers and mangy deer heads. His father's guns were locked away in the cellar, but Walter never played with those.

She recalled one of Walter's early complaints: that his father had never taken him hunting. His father had used to joke that Walter would accidentally shoot himself, or that he would faint if he saw a deer killed. His father had probably been right.

Even though Katy liked swimming in chill water, she could stand it today for only fifteen minutes. She was shivering when she climbed onto the dock and wrapped herself tightly in a thick, oversized towel. When she entered the living room, she found Walter surrounded by an arsenal.

"You shouldn't swim naked like that, hon," he said before she could speak. "Anybody could see you."

"Oh, Walter! From the other side of the lake? Anybody who wants to go to the trouble of watching me with binoculars is welcome."

She couldn't resist adding maliciously: "I think they're too close when I find them masturbating in my bedroom closet."

The jibe didn't bother him. He said, "That rapist is still loose, you know. For all you know, he's on this side of the lake."

"I'm sure you'll protect me, dear. You certainly have enough hardware to do it. What is all this?"

"Just looking at my father's guns, that's all. Don't look so worried. They aren't loaded."

In the next instant, she nearly gave herself away. She was on the verge of reminding him that he'd told her the pistol at home wasn't loaded, either. She caught herself just in time, but the near-lapse left her shaking.

"See this?" He held up what looked like a double-barreled shotgun. "It's an express rifle. It fires a slug the size of a banana on an absolutely flat trajectory for a couple of hundred yards. You could stop a truck with it."

"That's nice," she said abstractedly, hugging herself. "Would you like a drink?'"

"No, I got to go back to the store and make a phone call. You want anything?"

"Why didn't you make it on the way here?"

"Well, I forgot. It's nothing important, just something I should've done at the office today, that's all."

She glanced at the clock. It was eight-thirty already. "Oh, I forgot to tell you, dear. *The Big Sleep* is on the tube tonight. It starts at nine. You shouldn't want to miss that."

"Gee, no, hon, I'd better run. That's great. Thanks, I would've missed it."

"We haven't even eaten yet, Walter. Can't you make your call tomorrow?"

"It won't wait. I can grab a sandwich while I watch the film," he said, hurrying out.

Damn him and his damned phone call! He had just put the first snag in the plan. He'd had a drink back at the house, one here at the lodge. He was cold sober, and it was unlikely that she could pour enough liquor into him before nine-thirty to convince a pathologist that he'd been drunk. Well, she could head off Frank and give Walter another hour of drinking time. It would increase the risk that Frank's car, might be seen under the bridge, but that was a very slim risk to start with.

The movie started without him, and she watched it blindly as her agitation grew. He wandered in at ten after nine and looked at the screen for awhile, accepting the stiff drink she gave him without a word. Then, exasperatingly, he rambled off to the kitchen.

He returned in a little while with a butcher knife, which he began to sharpen methodically and irritatingly on an oilstone.

"Carve enough for me, too, will you?" she said.

"Enough what, hon?"

She looked at him sharply. He was grinning to himself.

"I presume you're doing that so you can make a ham sandwich."

"A ham sandwich," he repeated. "Sure thing, hon."

She watched the movie, or pretended to, while Walter's gritty task proceeded. At last he stood up. He moved in front of her chair. With his knife, he flicked the hem of the towel she still wore. The towel parted easily.

"Walter!"

"Have you ever thought it would be sexy to be undressed by a guy with a knife? I mean, like he would cut your clothes off, piece by piece?"

"No, I haven't, and we're missing the movie. Sit down and have a drink."

He feinted with the knife. She put her hands up and screamed. He slipped the knife between her breasts and jerked outward, slicing the towel. He pulled the shreds away from her.

"Stop it, Walter, stop it!" she shouted. "What the hell

are you doing?"

"You look better naked," he said, kneeling in front of her, staring at her nakedness with disconcerting intensity. She didn't dare move a muscle as he pressed the cold blade to her belly and slid the point into her pubic hair.

"I heard something funny on the radio at the store, whore." He giggled as he repeated: "The store, whore."

"Are you all right, Walter? You're acting very strangely, you know."

"It seems that the Full Moon Maniac has struck again. In broad daylight, this time."

She cringed back as Walter touched the point of the knife to one of her nipples. "Who was it?" she said, and her voice was a dry croak. "Did he kill anyone?"

"Sonny," he said.

"I don't understand. What is this all about? What has this got to do with us?"

"The reason they know is, Sonny was killed with the same gun that killed the other people. John Evans. Melody Boisvert. William Oates, Jr. Suzy Decker. Quentin Swift."

"They – Suzy and Quentin – they weren't shot."

"If they ever find the heads," Walter said, touching the knife to her throat, "they will find bullets in them."

The tears in her eyes made it hard for Katy to see the clock clearly, but she thought it said nine-twenty-five. She screamed as loudly as she could.

Chapter Fifteen

Frank lay soaking in a hot tub and listening to Walcha's old recording of *The Art of Fugue* on the college radio station. Every part of his body seemed to ache in a distinct and separate way, but the pain became unbearable only when he moved.

Considering his physical condition, he was in incredibly high spirits. He felt like someone who had just been granted a reprieve on the threshold of the execution chamber. Only now that killing Walter was out of the question did he realize what a mad scheme it had been. His love for Katy had blinded him. Sonny had done him an incalculable service by keeping him out of that trap.

He was surprised, and even a little disappointed, that the police hadn't come looking for him yet. He had almost looked forward to the challenge of undergoing an interrogation without revealing that he had been beaten within an inch of his life this afternoon. And it would be impossible to conceal that fact after tomorrow, when he would have to see a doctor, who would undoubtedly put his arm and shoulder in a cast.

He could see only one way of getting a convincing

explanation for the cast, and it was a drastic way. Later tonight he planned to go to the French Club, drink hard and fast for half an hour, and then make a loud remark about stupid Canucks. He had great confidence in Jean Ducrot, the bouncer, who was built like a chest of drawers. He knew that Jean would get to him first and try to hustle him out of the place. He would resist and Jean would clobber him, but the bouncer's main goal would be to get him out the door. It would be enough to account for his broken bones; unfortunately, it was likely that he would get a few more in the process.

On the way to the bar, he would get rid of the gun. Sonny's idea had been good enough: toss it off the Water Street bridge.

After that, his only worry was Katy's reaction to his aborting of the plot, but he didn't expect much trouble there: his injuries would speak for themselves. If, even so, she got nasty about it, he could point out that he wouldn't have needed to shoot Sonny with Walter's gun if she hadn't bitten his right hand.

Then they could fall back into their old game of thinking up ways to snuff Walter: This time he would make sure that it never became anything more than a game. Maybe, in thirty or forty years, he would agree to some plan like loosening a crucial nut on Walter's wheelchair.

He was still laughing aloud when the nine o'clock news came on. He soon stopped laughing.

He dressed quickly except for a shirt, then taped his right arm as tightly as he could to immobilize the elbow. He fashioned a sling for the arm out of a pillowcase. He took the Mag from its holster, checked the load, and put it inside the sling. He draped a bush jacket over his shoulders. As an afterthought, he took Walter's gun and stuck it in the left front pocket of his jeans.

Walter the Maniac. He couldn't quite deal with it. He still wanted Sonny to be the Maniac. He had been congratulating himself on having wiped out half of the rape-and-murder team, but he had only killed a screwy kid. Maybe Pa had let Sonny use his gun, the way Ma had let him use her chainsaw – no, it hadn't happened that way; it was Walter, it had always been Walter.

It took an effort to hold himself back from running to his car and speeding to the lake, but he knew that he should try to think it all through first. He was tortured by the thought that Katy was all alone' in an isolated spot with a homicidal madman. The knowledge that she had been married to the same homicidal madman for fifteen years, that they had been alone many times in the past, did nothing to ease the torture. After all, Walter's mania was getting demonstrably worse: he had progressed from rape to murder by gunshot, from there to murder by arson, from there to murder by decapitation. He was probably looking for a new kick. Katy might be it.

He thought of calling ahead to the state police or to the town constable at the other end of the lake. Neither would credit an anonymous tip that the distinguished Mr. Walter Burroughs was the Full Moon Maniac. But he wouldn't have to say that. He could simply say that something funny was going on at the lodge, that he'd heard a scream. Katy would have heart failure when they arrived; he estimated that either the constable or the state troopers would get there around nine-thirty, the time when he had been scheduled to arrive on the scene and snuff Walter. But he himself wouldn't be able to get there until ten-thirty at the earliest, and by that time . . .

By that time nothing would have happened. Walter's

movie would still be on. Walter would be a little drunker, that would be the only difference. He could still carry out the plan.

He was still trying to think through the difficulties that Sonny's death had caused when he was struck by a new and frightening thought: Walter must know by now that his gun had been stolen and used to shoot Sonny. The Full Moon Maniac was big news regionally. It didn't matter whether Walter was watching the movie on a channel from Hartford or Providence of Boston; they would surely have mentioned it in one of their short news summaries, or even interrupted the movie with a bulletin.

He ran down to his car without bothering to lock the door behind him and got underway, ignoring the pain it cost him.

His thoughts weren't much clearer when, forty-five minutes later, he parked his car beneath the wooden bridge that Katy had described. Having heard the news, Walter would know that somebody – whoever had shot Sonny – knew his secret. He would be scared, and his fear might drive him to irrational violence. If he had discovered his gun missing and made a fuss about it, he might suspect that Katy had figured out his secret. Worst of all, he might suspect her of having taken it and given it to whoever had shot Sonny.

He climbed back to the gravel road and ran. The jolt of each step transferred itself through his spine to his injured shoulder and arm. The Colt kept bouncing against his elbow in the sling. He stumbled once and twisted his ankle. He reminded himself sternly that he had never fainted in his life.

Past the rail fence, he bad to move more slowly through the overgrown meadow. The night was overcast, and he had trouble following the ill-defined path in the dim glow of diffused starlight. The meadow was loud with frogs and crickets, but occasional scurryings in the underbrush sounded even louder. He drew his pistol twice before convincing himself that he had heard only some small animal.

Among the tall trees at the top of the slope, the gloom was impenetrable. He might have been standing in an unlighted cathedral. He paused in the hope that his eyes would accustom themselves to the darkness, but they didn't.

He moved ahead. As Katy had assured him, there was no underbrush. The wood was, thickly carpeted with needles from the tall trees. There were rocks, though. He tripped over one and fell sprawling on his injured arm. He screamed aloud, but he was able to cut the cry short.

When he could stand, he realized that his pistol had fallen out of the sling. He scuffed his feet around in a widening circle, but he couldn't find it.

He stood up straight and looked ahead. He knew he was going in the right direction because, far ahead, he could see the lights of the summer bungalows across the lake. But he saw nothing at all where he imagined the lodge lay. None of the houselights she had promised was on. It was all too easy to picture a madman brooding in darkness over Katy's lifeless body.

He reached into the pocket of his jeans for his key-ring. He had to slip his hand past Walter's pistol. The touch of it gave him a feeling of revulsion. He had to remind himself that it was only steel, only a gun. He fished out his key-ring with its penlight. His own Colt lay ten feet away. He retrieved it and returned it to the sling. He noted the time: ten-thirty already. He fanned the light around him and saw the path he should have been following. He returned to it, snapping the light off but keeping it ready in his hand.

Maybe Katy had encouraged Walter to drink to his

limit in time for his nine-thirty appointment. Some time after that, he had passed out. She had put him to bed and perhaps gone to bed herself, turning all the lights off as a sign that the plan was to be cancelled.

That was a plausible explanation, but Frank didn't believe it.

If Walter was there, Walter was going to die.

He couldn't shoot him with the gun that had killed Sonny, nor could he shoot him with the Mag. He could take him out to the lake and drown him, though. Walter was bigger than he, and a few years younger, but Frank didn't doubt that he could overpower him with one arm. He pictured himself taking Walter's lower lip ungently between his thumb and forefinger in the come-along hold he'd used as a patrolman on drunks and whores, hurrying him into the lake and holding him down. He doubted that Walter was a competent swimmer. He might be able to drown him without leaving a mark on his body.

What difference did it male? Katy was dead. Yes, and so were Melody Boisvert and Suzy Decker, and that's, why Walter was going to die. If Katy was dead, he had nothing at all to lose. Maybe he would go after Ma Corcoran next.

He almost ran into the side of the house before he saw it. It was a big, half-timbered structure, a Victorian barn in Elizabethan style. Both back doors were locked. He hurried around to the gravel apron in front. No car. The front door was locked. He smashed a front window with his gun and raised it.

Inside, the lights worked. The living room was in disarray. A chair had been overturned, a whiskey bottle lay on the floor. Rifles, pistols, and shotguns, about fifteen weapons in all, lay around the room.

The TV set was still warm, and that detail enraged him. If he had left his home fifteen minutes earlier, or if he had driven straight to the front of the lodge upon arriving – but such thoughts were worse than useless.

He made a fast but thorough search of the lodge from attic to cellar, checking under every bed and in every closet. He didn't find Katy. He didn't find any bloodstains, either.

He hesitated in the living room, staring at the collection of pistols. He could take a gun of Walter's that wasn't identifiable as a murder weapon and work some improvised variation of the original plan. He rejected the idea. He had been clever enough for one night. If he ran into Walter, he would blast hire with whatever came to hand.

On his way out the back door, he grabbed a big flashlight he had seen before and used it as he raced up the path.

Fury and instinct got him as far as town and the Burroughs, house on High Street. He had just forced the front door of the dark and empty house when reason began to reassert itself. He could accomplish nothing by chasing around in circles. He had no idea where Walter had taken Katy, or where he might take her. Maybe up to one of the dirt roads or firelanes around Mt. Amos, the center of the previous murders – but that thought only emphasized his helplessness. It would take him a week to scour the hills on his own.

He went to Walter's study and called police headquarters. Captain LaPlante was still in his office.

"Captain, this is Frank Buchanan. I have reason to believe that Walter Burroughs is" – he stopped, realizing that he couldn't prove what he'd intended to say – "that he's gone berserk. He's taken his wife off someplace, and I think she's in serious danger. He's probably armed."

Into the long silence that followed, Frank said: "Captain?"

At last LaPlante sighed and said, "Frank, I don't know if this is what you'd call a strange coincidence, or if some people have gotten together and decided to dump a bunch of horseshit on my head for their own reasons. Where are you, Frank?"

"What difference does that make? And what the hell are you talking about?"

"Look, Frank, not five minutes ago Mr. Burroughs called me up to say that his wife had been kidnapped from their house at Painter Lake. He heard her screaming and ran downstairs in time to see you dragging her out the door. When he tried to stop you, you flashed a snub-nose .38. Then you barreled off in a red convertible."

"He doesn't even know me, for Christ's sake!"

"He says he does. He says you've been annoying his wife for the past month or so, making a real pain in the ass out of yourself. He was going to report it to us, but she convinced him that she'd cooled you off. Now, where are you?"

"I'm in Armitage. Look –"

"Well, if you are, that blows his story all to hell, unless you snatched her with a helicopter. Why don't you prove it by taking a stroll down to headquarters and showing us your ugly face?"

"Captain, you've got to put out an all points for him, I'm sure he's going to kill his wife, if he hasn't already. He called you to set me up for it. I was at his house at the lake looking for him an hour ago, and he wasn't there, but he left half an arsenal lying around the place. I bet he had the other half with him."

"Tell me where you are, Frank. I'll send somebody around for you, then we can talk about it."

"I'm looking for Walter. I'm at his house on High Street now. I just – there, I just stopped the electric clock on his desk at eleven-forty-five, which is the time now. I'll leave his front door standing open, so the boys can walk in and check what I just said. I won't be here."

"Don't pull this Sherlock Holmes shit on me, Frank! The only way you can get me to listen to you –"

Frank hung up and ran out the back door. He knew where Katy was. He hoped Walter would still be there, too.

He hurried down the ravine where he'd killed Sonny. He couldn't take his car; the goddamned thing was too conspicuous. If he got out of this alive, he planned to trade his car for the drabbest sedan he could find.

He ran down Railroad Avenue to Water Street, where he slowed his pace to a walk. Nearing his apartment, he didn't see anything that looked like a stakeout. He didn't see Walter's car, either.

He stopped opposite his garage. The lights upstairs were on, but he'd left them on when he'd hurried out. The bays of the garage were empty. He was certain that Walter liked the trick he'd pulled before so well that he planned to do it again: by dumping Katy's body in his apartment. He'd announced his intention this time, though, by calling the police to make sure they got the point.

He scanned the street quickly. He saw the shadow of a husky pedestrian who might have been a cop, but he was walking away. Frank moved quickly across the street, pulling Walter's gun from his pocket.

He crept up the stairs. The door at the top was ajar. He hesitated, then remembered he'd left it that way. He almost laughed aloud. He'd given lectures on protecting the home from intruders: the first rule, always lock your door.

He kicked the door open and went in low, moving the gun fanwise before him, almost shooting Katy by reflex, changing direction quickly and ending up on one knee with his back tight against the wall.

One of his chairs had been turned to face a corner. She sat in it, her hands tied behind her, head slumped forward. He couldn't tell if she was alive. He kept searching the room with his eyes.

"Katy."

She answered with only a muffled grunt. She had been gagged. But she was alive! He began to tremble. He couldn't prevent his head from turning toward her.

That was when Walter stepped out of the clothes-rack and smashed the gun out of his hand.

Frank stared into twin barrels of impressive dimensions. Walter had used the weapon to bat the gun from his hand. It was numb. He couldn't flex his fingers completely.

"What the hell is that thing?" Frank said.

Walter giggled. "An express rifle. It can blow the spine out of an elephant. Imagine what it can do to you."

"Tell you what, Walter. My right arm is broken and I think you just did the same for my left hand. Put it aside and I'll wrestle you for it."

"You don't understand. We aren't playing games, I don't play games with swine like you. I'm here to kill you. – Stand up and face the wall, spread your legs, you know how cops do it, don't you?'

"Sure," Frank said, doing as he was told. "But wouldn't it make more sense to shoot me first and search me later?"

"We have an hour to kill. A little less, actually. I only just called the police and told them how you'd kidnapped my wife."

Walter bossed him like a television cop, patting his pockets delicately. He didn't even touch the sling where the .357 Magnum Colt Python was concealed.

"What happens in an hour?" Frank asked.

"You can turn around now," Walter said, and Frank tried not to show the relief he felt as he took the weight off his bruised hand. "Good. I want to tell you to your face. I plan to shove this elephant gun up Katy's cunt and pull both triggers. Then I plan to shoot you with the .45 in my pocket – the outraged husband, arriving on the scene a split second too late."

"Walter, I'm not a crazy sexual-deviate, like you. Why would I do a thing like that?"

As he had hoped, Walter smashed him across the face with the gun-barrels. But he did it too quickly for Frank to grab them.

"You have to speak respectfully to me, pig. Don't call me Walter. It's Mr. Burroughs. But to answer your question, in case you haven't guessed, you're the Full Moon Maniac. There's the gun. You used it to kill Raymond this afternoon."

"Yeah, but it's your gun."

"Prove it. I bought it illegally, years ago. No records, no serial number, nothing."

Frank didn't want to talk to Walter; he wanted to pull out the Mag and blow him away. But he had to make absolutely sure his hand would obey him, first. He kept forcing his fingers to bend.

"Anyway, Walter, all this big talk about killing is just a lot of crap. Ma always did the killing, didn't she?"

"I told you, don't call me Walter!"

"Toot-toot!" Frank hooted.

He thought he'd pushed too far for a moment. Instead of swinging the gun at him and giving him another chance to seize it, Walter stepped back and raised it to point directly at his head.

"Do you know something, pig? I wouldn't have cut the Decker whore's head off if she hadn't said that to me. After I finished with her, she made that noise. So I got the chainsaw out of the back of the car. And I started it up. And I told her exactly what I was going to do. And she didn't make that noise anymore; she started screaming." He giggled. "I guess you could say she screamed her head off."

"Well, if you're going to cut my head off, you'd better call up Ma and ask if you can borrow the chainsaw. But the chances are she doesn't love you anymore. If she heard the news, she probably thinks you shot Sonny. I know I wouldn't want her thinking that about me."

Walter stared at him for a while, a giant, quizzical mole. Then he laughed. "I know what you're trying to do. I mean, you're trying to push me into doing something stupid. You think I'm dumb. You think I'm some kind of fucking half-wit, like Raymond." He laughed harder. "You can't do it! Christ, what a sense of power this gives me! Make that noise again, go on, do it! I can take it. I'm better than you are. I'm going to kill you. In twenty minutes you'll be dead, and I'll be alive, and Katy will be a red paste all over your fucking ceiling. Say, 'toot-toot,' asshole, if that makes you feel better."

"I'd rather call you Walter. That seems to get to you more."

"You can't touch me. Say anything you want to. It's only words, only breath, and I'm going to stop your breath."

"Fuck it, you've taken all the fun out of it," Frank said. "What did you do with the heads?"

"You've seen too many bad movies," Walter said, "where the killer gets the drop on the detective and encourages him to talk about his crimes, and then someone comes in the door and saves the day. Real life isn't like that. But to answer your question, I emptied the gun into her head. Then I cut off Swift's head and used it for target practice, too. Swift's head wasn't as good; it came all apart. Then I threw the heads down a privy on an abandoned farm outside of town."

"Do you mind if I take Katy's gag off, and go over to see how she is?"

"She's the same as ever. If you take her gag off, she'll scream."

"Maybe she'd like to contribute to this brilliant conversation."

"There's only one thing her dirty mouth is good for, and it isn't talking. Do you want to screw her? It'll be your last chance."

"Somehow I don't feel sexy at the moment. I thought it was Ma who liked to watch people. And kill them. I never thought a scumbag like you could do it."

He laughed. "You're trying to do it again. Keep trying. I won't kill you till I'm ready. As for Ma, she got tired of watching. She wanted that Evans kid to screw her. Just when he was grunting, when he started coming, I sneaked up behind him and put a bullet in his head. You should've seen the look on Ma's face. I wish I'd had a camera."

"Ma didn't kill anybody?"

"She had a sawed-off shotgun, just like the one Vince Edwards used in *The Killing,* but she never used it."

The mess that had been Walter's head only a split second before splashed all over Frank as a deafening roar filled the room. Ma stood in the door with the sawed-off shotgun, her face dead white, her mouth working soundlessly. The look in her bulging eyes would have given a rattlesnake nightmares. He now knew the identity of the husky pedestrian he'd spotted. She must have been watching Walter's house and shadowed him here.

Frank dropped even as Walter's body hit the floor. A second blast ripped a hole in the wall where he had just been standing. He succeeded in pulling the Mag from his sling as Ma pumped a third round into the chamber. His first shot missed her completely. The second hollow-point slug demolished her. The third that he fired into her jerking body was unnecessary.

"But what the hell," he said, getting to his feet and hitting her with the fourth, fifth, and sixth rounds.

He shoved the gun into his belt and went to Katy. Walter had put a pillow behind her head and covered her nakedness with a blanket, so she could wait in comfort for her execution. She was shaking. He jerked the tape quickly from her mouth and went to work on Walter's clumsy but effective knots.

"You're wonderful!" she croaked. "When you didn't come to the lake – when I was tied up, with Walter telling me all the dirty little details of what he'd done – Christ, I think I hated you more than him! I thought you'd chickened out. I thought you were a coward and a weakling and –"

"Save the pretty compliments," he said as he heard distant sirens converging on the place. "Let's get the hell out of here."

"You idiot! Don't you realize you've just solved the case?" she cried as he dragged her to her feet. "I heard Walter confess; I saw what happened. I'll swear I let you take his gun because you suspected him and wanted to have a ballistics comparison made. Nobody is going to worry about you shooting a creep like Sonny."

Frank thought about Sonny Corcoran. He thought about his painful struggle to rise above his rotten origins. He thought about how he had given Sonny provocation for the final attack.

"I'll worry about Sonny," he said.

www.ingramcontent.com/pod-product-compliance
Lightning Source LLC
Chambersburg PA
CBHW020614310726
48979CB00008B/1473/J